Unbanging the Nails

Unbanging the Nails

Richard Hillesley

for Sue

Enjoy

Richard

Unbanging the Nails was first published in 2019
By Clochoderick Press

A collection of stories of life as she is lived, and not a record of
fact. The characters and events in this collection are fictional,
and do not represent any real event or person, living or dead.

Clochoderick Press
Flat 4
8 Townhead Terrace
Paisley
Renfrewshire
Scotland
PA1 2AX

A CIP catalogue for this book is available from the British
Library
ISBN: 978-1-912345-10-6

Typeset by Mairibeth MacMillan in Palatino Lintotype

Printed and bound by
Imprint Academic
Seychelles Farm, Upton Pyne, Exeter, Devon, EX5 5HY

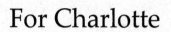

For Charlotte

Unbanging the Nails

Seacoal

We stayed on a stone farm up the coast from here. Dogs in the yard, wet cowpats and hay. It rained all week, filled the air with the stench of damp earth and silage. Stone walls and bent trees. Swill of the becks through the weeds and twisted roots, pebbles and circling pools. Over the tops of the greygreen hills the clouds swirled and the trees shivered.

We met a man down there on the black sands when the tide was out, shifting among the pools, rock spills and seawrack, with a grey sack in his hand. Cloud drift. White line of the sea. The man was scavenging for seacoal. We watched him from the trees, whispering and wondering who or what he was, a slow shadow lurching across the sands with a small dog at his heels.

He moved towards a shed under the cliffs, motionless and timeless, and stood there, still as stone. We threw things into the waves and looked away. The tides whooped and the skies drifted. The dog sniffed around us and barked. The sea was loud, breaking and cold. He shouted to us and called us over. He had a fire going. Thin twists of smoke blew into the sky.

We sat in his shack and watched him. Outside, the wind knocked on the roof. He looked at the wall, silent and coughing, and chewed his lip. His face was cracked and dotted like a piece of old china. He was blown by the wind, thrown up by the sea. And we loved it, his solitude and contrariness. When he spoke it was a distant rumour, rolling up from his belly.

- They won't move me,

1

he said, and we knew what he meant. His stark face cut away, landslides, crags and screes. We didn't see all that, his loneliness or pain. That is with you anyway. We loved him for being nothing, alone, a piece of this earth.

- That's Tommy,
they said at the farm.
- He's been that way since the strike.

The strike was two years over and lost. The day the men went back to work the whole village had marched on the pit. The women led with the banner, bright in their anger, and the men followed in silence, with bait and togs. The sky was filled with an eerie light and the thin streets echoed to the band as the men played the marching tunes, and the kids and the old folk waited on the corners and shouted,
- Wey Joey, quicken your step.
- Haddup, lads.
- We're proud on yis,
and clapped a sad distant sound like a storm over the hills.
At the top of Sedge Hill, the people gathered for the speeches. Thomas Houghton got up first. He stood there on the back of Eddie's lorry, disconsolate and uneasy, in front of the microphone. He stooped over and blew into it, looking faintly ridiculous, but no-one laughed. They didn't even speak.
- Lads,
he kept saying,
- Lads,
his legs apart, at a loss for words, he hung his head low on his thick neck.

- You've been magnificent, lads.

Silence filled the air, because nobody felt magnificent, and the emotion was too strong. Someone grabbed the microphone and shouted:

- We will never be defeated.

And Tommy stood firm at the back of the crowd and shouted,

- Scabs. Don't gan back.

But they ignored him.

- Scabs,

he shouted. And one of the women went to him and tried to tell him that it wasn't like that, that there were the bairns to think of, that they had been without pay for a year or more.

- Don't blame us, for we are not the ones,

she said. Her worn face had the lines etched into it like scar tissue, chiselled lines behind the careful kindness in her eyes, her eyes on fire, like slow burning coals. But he couldn't see it the way that she said it was. He could see no pride in lying down. He could see no victory in defeat.

- A'd rather starve than gan back,

he said. And she was angry and could not find the words, and said,

- Yir daft, man.

But it wasn't like that, for all that he could see was the inevitability of the rain and the cloudfilled sky, and the dark foreboding in the terraces on the hill, the grey damp light of day, and the smoking trees on the horizon.

- We have lost more than that,

he said.

- It's not about a job or having the clout to buy new clothes, and it's not about being decent for they've killed all that.

3

When they have us beaten we may as well be dead. A'm not gan back.

And he didn't go back. He walked to the top of Sedge Hill and stood beneath the high clouds and the grey line of trees, and turned and looked down across the streets falling away into the distance, where the men and their friends and families walked towards the pit gates, behind the brass and drums of the band, the ancient banner held high with its picture of the pithead as it was fifty years ago.

He could hear them singing, a distant echo between the house-ends, like fools, he thought, as he saw the valley below, with the pit and the grey hills, and the rain that fell through the ragged sky. He felt the wind and the chill on his face and the hard skin of his hands.

And he took himself up beyond the farm and the wind-blown trees. And on the black hill, he sat on a crop of rock, looking out to sea, and wept where no-one could hear his sobs, clenching his hands into his face and crying like a bit bairn. He stood up, swaying, and stamped his feet into the cold earth in frustration, and shouted,

- Bastards,

at the top of his voice, and waited as if the sound might echo back through the wind.

The Sunday after they went back, Tommy walked into the church during the service. He walked in noisily in his big bodied way, banging into the benches and scraping the floor with his boots when he sat down. This was the first many had seen of him since they went back and heads turned. But he sat in silence in his jacket and scarf, staring ahead of him, his lips pursed and his brow lined with deep gouges like spade

4

marks in a hard soil.

Their singing split the atmosphere, falling down the back of the verses and rising into the chorus just before the organ, hung notes spilt on empty air. They held the hymn books open in their hands, mouthing the words if they would not sing, until the echo of the organ stopped and they sat down uncomfortably on the hard pews, coughing and scraping and shuffling their feet as the vicar's high voice broke through the silence.

- Brothers and sisters,

he began, his hands on the lectern, his eyes peering out across the rows of faces fragile with emotion. He wanted to say what he felt, that he had been choked by what he had seen during the long months of the strike, and spoke slowly so that his words could be heard echoing and ringing against the cold stone walls and floor of the church, defying the silence as they echoed back towards him, clear as water, the flow disturbed by a slow rumble like distant thunder from Tommy in the back row.

- You are not my brother,

he said.

- And a'm not yours.

And the people in the polished wooden rows pretended not to hear the dark murmur of his voice rising from the back of the church. They coughed guiltily or they pulled out handkerchiefs and blew their noses. The vicar, distracted by the disturbance, peered through the strands of dim light that poured through the high windows, his head held high over the spectacles on his nose.

He lifted his fist to his mouth to stifle a cough, and told of his pride on the day of the return to work, when he had followed behind the banner and listened to the speeches of the men, and of how proud he had felt to be walking with such fine and dignified men and women. And now, he said, the battle was over, and the time had come to forgive and forget the bitterness and the hurt of the strike, to rebuild their lives and their community. The most difficult part was yet to come.

And Tommy, standing in the light cast from a window at the rear of the church, broke the silence again.
- Rubbish,
he murmured, with his hands on the seat back in front of him and a calm assurance in his eyes. He ignored the tutting and the turning of heads. These were not his people anyway.

The vicar coughed and pushed his hand through his falling hair. He fixed his gaze on the ones in the front row who wanted to hear what he had to say and who came back every week. Though he was nervous, he straightened his body, clutched the lectern more tightly, and focused on the text. His words that were somehow empty, even to himself, seemed to echo hollow through the air.

And Tommy spoke, too, from the back of the church, his low voice arching under the booming roof, colliding with the vicar's high soft consonants.
- What's God got to do with it anyway? God is with the police and the government. God is not with us. God has given us nowt that we haven't had to get down on our knees and beg for. We struck for wa jobs, not for charity. A'll not beg for me job. A'll not live on me knees.

This was too much for some of them, and they took Tommy by the arms and pushed him outside. Marie and Johnnie Stanhope and Hughie Gallagher and Jacka and Elaine

Smithson. They tried to reason with him. The vicar had meant well and he had been good to them throughout the strike, and their church had died like the pits and the strike. It wasn't their fault that no-one had stood by the miners. It wasn't their fault that the people couldn't see reality and wouldn't stand up for themselves. They'll regret it, they would say to each other, but they couldn't fight everybody else's battles if they wouldn't get up and fight for themselves, could they?

But Tommy wasn't listening. He wasn't having any of that. The Union men had been down and tried to persuade him to go back to work before his job was taken away, but he wouldn't.
- They won't move me,
he said,
- A'm not gan back,
and he hadn't. He had torn up his union card, and stood outside the colliery gates every day, holding a sign that he had made himself and carried throughout the strike.
- Keep up the fight,
was all it said. And that was how he felt.
- If we give in now, they will take everything from us. They won't be happy until we are gone forever, and they don't care what it costs, because it is never them that pays,
he said. John Stanhope and Jacka held Tommy's arms. Jacka had Tommy's neck pinned to the wall by his forearm, but still Tommy yanked and pulled and struggled until he pulled himself free from the sleeve of his jacket.
- A'll not give in,
he said. And Elaine said,
- See some sense, Tommy. Please, it's not worth it.

But Tommy had always been wilful. Even as a child he had

refused to take the cane for smoking when he hadn't been.
- A didn't do it,
he said,
- And you'll not hit me.

The teacher sent him home, and Tommy wouldn't go back. His dad beat him, his mother pleaded with him, the school board man and the social workers said they would put him into care, but he stayed away from school until the teacher had said he was sorry, and he went back to school a hero.

Marie and Jacka begged and cajoled him, and Elaine took him by the hand and walked him down the avenue. She, slight and gentle, tugging at his broad frame as she led the way. She said,
- There's nothin' we can do, Tommy. They have us over a barrel. If the men had stayed out we would have starved. So they've gone back, and we are dead anyway, but there's the bairns and we've got to eat. It's no use taking the fight to us.
- It's not you,
he said,
- It's all of us. They think they are the barons, and we are the serfs, and nothing has changed in a thousand years. We have to show to them it has.

Six weeks later, he had an eviction notice from British Coal. The union said they would help him but he didn't want to know. He knew the smell of his village. He knew the smell of his home. He walked the streets into the hills and down to the sea to keep himself busy during the day, and didn't waste his time thinking about British Coal or his rent.

The darkening clouds wrapped rings around the skyline, lifting light skirts of smoke, slag faeces heaped on higher hills, further away. A slow wind. The pit-cage shook, knocked the rim of the well. A weed shivered in a fence-crack. In the yards the trucks were quiet, and the hard rails flaked with rust. The stone streets were riveted into the sides of the hills. A silver Cortina with a rust-coloured door and a van without a tax disc. Two kids playing football.

- He thinks he's Peter Beardsley,

said one of them, and it was true that the other had the same orphan boy face with the open mouth and lost hairstyle, and he balanced the ball on his toes and made a sliding tackle through the long grass, his too-long jeans hanging from his waist.

- Goal,

he shouted.

- 's not,

said the other,

- Went over the bar.

- Ha ha,

Tommy laughed, walking past.

He went home and sat on a chair in the upstairs room, looking out over the back lane, sheds and vegetable plots, listening to pop music on the radio as he always did when he wasn't out walking or listening to the rain.

He sketched the world differently from his window. A place of strict lines and dashes, broken images, clouds like wide strokes of a brush, splashes of colour hanging from the distressed washing lines between the diagonal poles and the hard edges of the outhouses and the disused sheds. Squares of light on the glass. The stiff-backed chair and the hard table.

A light wind ruffled the grasses and the shirts and dresses on the washing lines. A dog barked. And in next-door's yard, between the fence and the potting shed, he could see the pen where Bobby Wilson kept his fox, the poor bastard, penned into a shadowed yard, without space and light, and for nothing but show. Sometimes he could see it, pushing its nose against the wires, or the wooden bars of its cage, desperate for the soft earth of the fields and for clean air to breathe.

- I couldn't do that,

he said to himself.

He made a small pile in the back yard from boxes of rubbish and bits of furniture, and each day he would add a little more. And the pile grew until it was higher than the back wall, and filled the yard from front to back. From his walks he brought back sacks of rubbish, over the shoulder of his Coal Board donkey jacket, and added them to the heap in his yard.

In the beginning the people said,

- Well, that's Tommy for you, mad bastard. Somebody should say something to him, and stop him carrying on that way.

Or they would say,

- What's the point in being angry with someone like that? He cannot help himself. It was his mum and dad's fault. They was always too hard on him. They never let him finish his schooling. They say he was bright at school. What a shame it is for him to have ended that way when he could have made something of himself and been somebody.

And some were a little afraid of him, for his strangeness. But he always talked straightforwardly when they spoke to him and seemed quite normal. And nobody was really bothered by him. They thought of saying something to the doctor and getting him to go down there on some other pretext, but they never did.

And what he said about it when someone asked was that, if British Coal could kick him out of his home, so he could make things difficult for them in his own small way. He said, - I want to be a pimple on the face of British Coal so each time they look in the mirror they feel bad and it spoils their day, no matter how much they pick and squeeze me. I will still be there, a pain on their faces.

And the people laughed at that. And the pile outside his house grew, and the strange thing was that not all of it was Tommy's rubbish. Other people were adding to the pile as some gesture of solidarity with Tommy and his rent trouble. There was no consolation for the breaking of the strike, but at least they felt a little better.

They threw beds onto the heap, old mattresses and car seats, boxes and prams, everything, and the mess began to spread out onto the street. And Tommy would have to climb over the mountain to get into his house. It was a stupid thing to do, but it was funny. And everyone felt better for it, more a part of the community. The mountain was growing day by day, a strange peak beneath the heap of Sedge Hill, topped by a decaying armchair and a standard lamp. The street balanced along the green and grey slope of Sedge Hill, a line of black trees at the top, Tommy's heap between the house-ends.

After a month or two, the bailiffs came. They came with a van and two police cars but it wasn't enough. When the people saw them coming they went to bring their neighbours and came out onto the street. They jeered and shouted, and when Tommy emerged from the front door, half-hidden by the rubbish, he had become a hero and they cheered him for his audacity and bravery. He argued but the bailiffs emptied his house, and everything the bailiffs removed, the people picked up and returned.

Tommy was taken into custody and they brought more bailiffs, but the crowd kept growing, and they could not be tamed. They barricaded both ends of the street, and more police arrived.

At the end they had taken everything of Tommy's and put it into safe keeping and the bailiffs got nothing. They pulled up the floorboards and carpets and piled them onto the heap and set the mess on fire. It burnt all night, and, in the chaos, Bobby Wilson's fox got away.

There was a party until six in the morning and everyone crawled into their beds with a warm glow. And Tommy saw none of it. But the police charged him anyway, with affray and contempt and assault and battery, as they would, though it was Tommy that had the bruises. And when he was freed there was a crowd to see him out, and he was embarrassed. And when they said to him,
- What are you going to do, Tommy?
he said,
- A want to be a pimple on the face of the coalboard,
and they laughed.

But he didn't find another place to live. Instead, he built a shack down on the beach, which was British Coal property. He had a bed and a Calor Gas stove, which was all he needed, and collected seacoal to sell to the farmers and the visitors to the village.

On our last day, we walked down by the cliffs. The sea was cold and breaking. Sun glance on a gull's wing. Tufts of grass shuddering in a gasp of wind. You could smell the rain that was coming. The wind lifted and the grasses shivered. It was cold down there.

His dog saw us first, and came running rings around us and barking at our heels. Tommy looked up and offered us tea, and we sat crouched in his shack, smoking strings of Golden Virginia. He said that the men had been from British Coal to move him on, but he wouldn't go.
- A'm staying put,
he said, smiling.

We asked him about the strike, and then about the eviction. And he liked to tell us, maybe because we were young and strangers to the village. His back straightened as he talked, and you could hear the pride in his voice as he took us through the history of the pits and the union and his house burning down. And he told us,
- While they was going mad round my house, making noise and fighting, a crept out and went next door, and took the fox he kept and set it free. Don't tell them that though.

And he laughed with teeth broken like a fence, a tab on his bottom lip, and a wisp of smoke in the pits of his eyes.

Richard Hillesley

The Wind and the Cow

We rocked up on Iona from Fionnphort in a swell in an open boat. A petrel skimmed the waves. Salt and spray tipped over the gunnels. A storm was on its way. The wind was lifting and the gulls swirled over the scraps thrown into the water from a fishing boat wallowing in the sound. A man on the landing smiled at us and asked if we were looking for God. We could only say,
– No.
But we were looking for a place to pitch our tent.
– You'll find him here,
he said.
– Up there,
he said, pointing to a row of tents near the Priory.
Iona was a thin place, a strand of light between land and sea, a tuft of grass on the edge of the ocean, three and a half miles long and one mile wide. You could smell religion and its ghosts in the wind. You could feel it in the stone.

We pitched our tent in the field near the Priory and walked to the Bay at the Back of the Ocean. The sand was made of shells and the light was soft and pagan.
– like daylight through a pub window,
said Alice.
The beach and sand were a flowering at the edge of the sea. Stiff grass and silt where the curlews picked and strutted in the swash and drift of the tide. The clouds rolled across the horizon. The waves were long and slow.
We walked back to the field and lay in our tent and listened

to the sound of the wind. Our dreams were of each other and the slap of the wind against the poles, and we didn't stir until one of the young Christians from the abbey put his head around the flap of our tent.

– Hey,

said Alice,

– You can't do that.

But he didn't seem to notice.

– Pack up your tent and come to the Chapter House, he said.

– We're having all night prayers and a talk on the war in Ireland.

Columba fought a war in Ireland. He went to war over the right to own a book. His enemy was Diarmait mac Cerbaill who decreed, 'To every cow belongs her calf. To every book belongs its copy', and thus denied Columba the right to keep the copy he had made of the Psalter of St Jerome. The book was made of vellum. Vellum was made of calf skin. Columba took his revenge at the battle of Cúl Dreimhne in County Sligo. Three thousand and one men fell in the battle over the right to own the book. Columba was a prince and a monk and a scribe. Diarmait mac Cerbaill was a King of Tara. Three thousand of the dead were followers of Diarmait. One was a follower of Columba. Columba was sent to Iona to pay penance for the slaughter, and brought Christianity to the Picts.

– Bring your sleeping bag. You can sleep on the floor, said the young Christian,

– There's a force nine gale on its way, and if you stay in your tent you'll be blown away.

15

We took him at his word. Not that we were afraid of the wind, but we hadn't had a bath in weeks. It was the possibility of a bed and a bath that tempted us to pack up our tent and go in search of a B&B among the upright and tidy houses of Iona. We asked in the shop and one of the women told us of someone who did that sort of thing on the other side of the village. By the time we got there she had been on the phone to warn that we were coming.

– I've heard about you,

said the woman, peering round her door.

– There's going to be a storm,

we said,

– and we need a bed for the night.

– You're not wearing a ring,

she said.

– Are you married?

– No,

said Alice.

– You can't stay here.

said the woman, and made as if to shut the door.

– But you can try Mrs McSweeney. She takes your sort.

By now the dark had closed in. And the wind was getting up. Mrs McSweeney had heard about us too.

– Do you have a room?

we asked, and she said,

- You can't stay in the house. But there is a barn.

The barn was a shed that may once have been a crofter's blackhouse, a homestead under a turf roof with living space at one end and a cattle byre at the other. The roof had been replaced with timbers and a covering of corrugated iron, and there was a dividing wall and a cow on the other side. The

dividing wall didn't reach to the roof.
– A pound a night in advance,
she said.
– Each.

There was a hurricane lamp, a high bedstead, a bunk bed against the opposite wall, no windows, an old school desk and a single chair. It was dry and clean, but there was straw on the floor and we could hear and smell the cow over the wall, and if we stood on tiptoe we could see it. After she shut the door, we hugged one another and laughed.
– Just like Joseph and Mary,
said Alice.

There was a rucksack and a violin case by the bunk bed and we realised we were not alone. We had a companion who turned up just as we began to settle in. He was bespectacled and shy and came from Germany. He sat at the desk and made notes in his journal by the flickering light of the hurricane lamp, and we lay on the bed with our books, and listened to each other. He was a young Christian and came to Iona every year and always stayed with Mrs. McSweeney. One year he had stayed in the back of a disused car in her yard and she had taken a pound a night from him, to stay in the car.

He didn't stay the night with us. He walked out into the wind with his shoulder bag and took his books to the Chapter House for prayers and a talk about the war in Ireland. On his way out, he popped his head around the door and said,
– Hello,
meaning to say goodbye. The wind howled through the door and we imagined him blowing down the lane as he walked to the Chapter House.

We lay on the bed in the barn and listened to the wind and the cow. The wind was worse than we had expected, and the rain was long and hard. The cow was unsettled and kept us awake through the night. Maybe it had been separated from its calf, or maybe it was the noise of the wind, rattling the edges of the roof and throwing things across the yard that disturbed the cow's equilibrium, but she wasn't quiet and she was not still.

The barn was like the barn in a painting by Marc Chagall. Harmonies in the colour and dissonance of bed and fiddle, paraffin lamp and Alice in her skirt over her jeans, and her walking boots that looked out of place. And the unexpected low of the cow that shook the walls.

Alice, rising off the bed, moved the chair to the dividing wall, stood on the chair and looked over the wall at the cow. A curious music went on between them. I looked over the wall and the cow flicked its tail and moo'd and Alice began to sing, a strange guttural song that echoed between the rafters as if she knew what the cow was feeling, with her arm hanging over the wall and the wind tearing at the roof.

I asked why she was singing but she ignored me and sang to the cow, and the cow moved towards her and licked her hand. The cow went calm and we went back to bed. They had found a harmony between them.

Columba didn't like women or cows. He once decreed: 'Where there is a cow there will be a woman, and where there is a woman there will be mischief,' and cows were banished from Iona to The Island of the Cows, and women were banished to The Island of the Women. Such was the symbolism of the woman and the cow.

And when we awoke in the morning, a thin light seeped across the sky and the air was oddly still, as if filled with guilt and remorse for the storm the night before. The storm had cleared the air. We washed under a tap in the yard, and followed our star to the south of the island and the Bay of the Buried Coracle, where we camped for a week, and left on the ferry one evening when the sun was hooked like a dying mackerel along the line of sea and sky.

On the wall above the urinal in the toilet next to the ferry landing someone had scrawled '*At this moment Iona is at the spiritual centre of the universe* – Mrs Mcleod, Iona Grocery store.'

Richard Hillesley

One Night of Sin

Laszlo came in. Smart tan shoes. He clutched the banisters at the bottom of the stairs and shouted up to his wife,
- Where are you?
I heard a muffled cry from upstairs. A door swung open and she yelled,
- How dare you? Where have you been?
And he walked back onto the street and slammed the door behind him. Windy prelude to another drunken evening. I could feel the ice under his shoes, the frost in his cranium, the screech in his liver. He was so meticulous. He shined every inch of his shoes, timed every rise and fall of his day, but his life was a mess.

That summer, we lived in the rooms below Laszlo and his wife and they turned our lives upside down. Laszlo didn't work because he couldn't. He didn't like being told what to do, and his pride wouldn't let him anyway. So he stayed at home and his wife earned the money. She was always at the end of her tether, stretched to the limit by his outraged sense of order, his face that fell in sudden hurt or raged in sullen anger for reasons that she could not predict or follow. But she wouldn't let you sympathise. She wouldn't let you know. At two in the morning one night, just after we had moved in, we heard her leaning out of the window yelling,
- He's killing me. He's killing me.
And someone down the street called the police, more from frustration and anger than concern for her. A police car came shrieking down the street with its siren blaring, and we lay in

our bed and listened to the knocking and banging and raised
voices as the doors above us opened and shut. After the police
left, she kicked our door and shouted,
- It's none of your business either.

He stayed in his room at the top of the house, and looked
down like a pilot on the world below. It was so simple from
up there. His room was his cockpit. He sat at his desk by the
window, his hand on the joystick, his eyes on the gauges, and
twisted and span through the clouds above. He could reach
in any direction for everything he wanted. Soaring above the
telegraph and thunder, he would sit with a pen in his hand,
lean to the left and sweep away the troubles of the world, lean
to the right and become master of all that he surveyed.

Laszlo was not like anyone else. He was afraid of the real
world and had built his own that was circumscribed by tidy
rules and unseen lines that he and you were not to cross, ley
lines across this house of rooms. And his room was stacked
with books and pens and ink and food and water. He had
collections of antique postcards and music, German helmets
and Marmite jars, coins and Ovaltine posters. A human
skeleton hung from the ceiling, its bones clanking in the
breeze from the window. And he soared through cirrus and
nimbus and into the silent wind above, Wagner or Elvis
stamping through the stacks and shaking the floor. The
neighbours banged on the walls and he shouted,
- Peasants,
and turned the volume higher, the music filling the gardens
and the street, Laszlo in the cockpit at the dormer window,
taking flight over the town and the fields, soaring through a
gap in the clouds, behind him his dinosaurs made from Airfix

kits, monsters in miniature with staring eyes, articulated legs and plastic armour plating, and the flocks of Airfix pterodactyls that hung on strings from the ceiling, like vultures circling over the leftovers on his dining table, their dark wings bent at the elbow, descending through the light air and falling onto the shadows below.

He made rules for others to live by, but he didn't live by them himself. He counted every unit of electricity that came into the house, his body hooked over the meter, a candle in his hand, watching the meter as it span around every time we had a bath or turned on a light. In his notebook he added the units used by me and Alice and himself and his wife, and when the bill came he paid almost nothing and said we were to pay the rest. One day I came out of the bathroom and caught him counting the units while I ran a bath.

- You're joking,

I said, standing on the landing with a towel around my middle.

- You're always having baths,

he said.

- So do you,

I said, and he said,

- I don't. When did I last have a bath?

And it was true. I hadn't seen or heard him going to the bathroom in all the time we had been there.

- I haven't had a bath for six months,

he said.

- Six months?

- It isn't good for you to wash too much...

he said,

- ... and it wastes electricity.

I couldn't argue because I didn't have it in me to watch him come and go. But a week or so later I saw him coming out of the bathroom door with his hair wet, and I wondered.

He was like that, his life measured by the clock in his head, every movement timed and noted, his intake of food and his body's responses written into a notebook for further reference. Laszlo was at the controls, his hands on the joystick and the throttle, and all else was superfluous or celebration until he had a drink to flush out his kidneys and the bad air from his lungs. Drink was his absolution, freed him from the chains of this earth, opened his wings and the dials span, and he soared through the clouds, absolved of guilt or responsibility.

And his wife dusted and cleaned around the skeletons and helmets, books and records, and coins and dinosaurs. She tidied up behind him, prepared his food, and made space for his flights of fancy into the stratosphere. One quiet Sunday afternoon I was lying on the bed covers, barefoot, reading a book, hiding in the shade from the humid heat of urban sunlight, when I heard their voices come ringing and clattering down the hollow stairs.
- You've dusted my dinosaurs,
he shouted,
- Of course I dusted your dinosaurs. They were dirty.
- I know they were dirty,
he said, followed by the slam of doors, and a clatter of plates from the kitchen, her refuge when the dust was flying.
- I thought you would be pleased.
- But why?
- They were dirty.
- Of course they were dirty. I wanted them dirty. It took me

years to get them that dirty. They are dinosaurs. They're sixty million years old. They're supposed to be dirty.

- You're joking,

she said. But she always surrendered to his logic with its bracketing parentheses and perverse divisions. He leapt the gap of reason and soared through the clouds, and she always listened, torn between her doubt and her wonder at his transformation of the world through words, so she was barely able to distinguish truth any more except through his eyes.

- You can't think that,

she would say, and he would say,

- That's the way it is.

And his affirmation persuaded her he must be right, even when she knew he wasn't. She let him rule her life like a child rules a parent, in fear of the remonstration and anger that turned her life inside out with plausible logic. Sometimes she rebelled, and the pots and pans banged the walls and clattered down the stairs in time to the music, and we would hear her yelling back,

- No, I won't,

And we wondered why she bothered, for we knew he wouldn't surrender. He would turn up the volume and blank out objection until she succumbed. And she always did, for the sake of peace, though a battle raged inside her. She was boiling under, and, though the lid rattled and there were gushes of steam, she suppressed her anger, and surrendered her will to him.

It couldn't last. Throughout that long, hot summer, we waited for the clouds to open and the storm to break, when the heavens opened, flooding the streets, her will crashing through his anger and her submissiveness gone, his plane riding down the side of the wind and crashing into the face of the Downs, his body pressed into the hillside, the Devil's Dyke or Wilmington Hill, humbled at last.

We waited through the warm colours and smells of summer, the salt sea air blowing up from the beaches, the light evenings as we lay on our bed with Elvis as our soundtrack, cutting with his oohaah words through the ceiling onto our lives. The music had no echo for me or for Alice. But what could we say? We knew that we would be moving out and probably wouldn't tell them. We moved to the music as if it wasn't there, merely a mood in the air that we could absorb and ignore until something better came along.

He invited us upstairs to listen to his music and see his boxes of truth, his books and his Marmite jars, all the sizes descending along the mantel-piece like a family of Marmite jars, and he spoke to me of the risen Elvis, the voice of an angel and the touch of the Holy Ghost, and when I said,
- Ah, but *Viva Las Vegas*,
- and those suits,
- and *Old Shep*,
- and those films,
- They're so bad.

He flicked his fingers back through his hair, and said,
- Yes, but Elvis was more than that. Listen to this,
and he played *Jailhouse Rock* with its gay come on lyric. And when I said,
- But he didn't understand what he was singing,
he was hurt and angry and said that it was a failing in me,

25

that I couldn't appreciate the obvious truth of Elvis, which I couldn't. He belonged to another world to mine, of America and the marketing of values like so much tinsel. Alice talked to his wife, Elaine, and I made signals across the room, with my eyes and my body, asking if she wanted to leave, but she ignored me and kept on talking. After, when I asked her why, she said,

- She makes me feel so good,
- Good?

I said,

- But I thought you didn't like her.
- I don't,

she said,

- She makes me feel good because I am not like her.

Not long after, they invited us up for a meal, and that was when it really began to go wrong. We came at half-past eight with wine and flowers. The lights were out. The room was lit by candles, and the table was laid. Elaine sat at the head of the table, and the air was stilted and confused.

- What do you think of the paintings of Hieronymus Bosch?

she said, out of the blue.

- Hieronymus Bosch?

I searched for an answer.

- Why?
- I don't like them,

she said.

- I'm not sure you're supposed to like them,

I said, lost for words or else bound to argue. So I was glad when Laszlo came into the room, dressed for the evening with a twitch and a swagger, his hair oiled back, sticky black,

in a careful quiff, his head nodding, his feet in two-inch thick black suede brothel creepers, topped off with a red velvet tuxedo, black pocket flaps and collar, a string tie and drainpipe jeans, the face, the lip, the voice.
- What do you think?
he said, and twitched across the floor.
- Elvis?
I said, though he looked more like a fifties' Ted.
- Yeah,
he said.
- Great,
I said, and I knew we were in for an evening with The King.
- You don't like Elvis, do you?
she said, and looked straight through me. They had been drinking and the air was brittle. Laszlo was already drunk, as I could tell by the way his arms swung behind the music. And she was angry.
- *Kissin' Cousins*,
I said,
- and Richard Nixon,
- and that badge that he gave him.
   And Laszlo picked up his guitar, moved back the chair, and began to play, knocking Elaine aside as she ladled the stew onto our plates.
- We're trying to eat,
she said, and he slurred the words of the song, spinning across the hardwood floor of their room, the polite rebel on a Bakelite radio between Joe Loss and the kitchen sink.
- The army,
I said to Laszlo.
- What about it?

27

Richard Hillesley

- He joined the army.
- He was drafted.
- He wasn't.
- He joined because the Colonel thought it was good for business.
- He did not.
- He joined for the Stars and Stripes.
- He did not,
he said. And he fell across the sofa to lift another record out of the rack, a glass of wine in his hand, his jacket spilling over the side. A record went on and the volume grew louder.
- Please. We're trying to eat.
Elaine said, and Alice laughed.
- Don't laugh. It only encourages him,
Elaine said. And the record came to an end, filling the room with an uncomfortable silence like the silence after rain, when the air is thick with dreams and things that are left unsaid.
- What have I done?
he said.
- You know what you have done,
she said.
- Why do you have to spoil everything?
   And he poured himself another glass of wine and choked and spat it out, and Elaine had to go to the kitchen for a rag. Her face was grim. The trenches were dug across the table. The knives and forks were drawn. And we could only wonder why they had asked us into their lives.
- *Wear My Ring Around Your Neck*,
I said.
- What?
- That was terrible,

28

I said. And he went,
- Oooh-ah-ha,
and Elaine threw up her arms, slammed her plate on the table,
and said,
- That's the end,
and headed for the kitchen, saying 'sorry' to Alice on the way
out. He sang a few bars of *Mystery Train*, ooh-aahed into the
stew, threw his guitar onto the floor, and muttered as he left
the room.

We could hear Elaine banging the pans in the kitchen on
the landing as we passed, and said our thank yous to her as
we went down the stairs. We tried not to notice the voice of
Elvis as he followed us to our room.

Come August we still hadn't moved out, having found
nothing we could afford in the right place at the right time,
and nothing we liked. We had resigned ourselves for the
moment to sharing our lives with Laszlo and Elaine, despite
the war in the upstairs flat. Wagner had become the theme of
the last few weeks, hard chords and strident voices crashing
down the stairs without a thought for us, followed by shouts
upstairs and dishes washed loudly, plate against plate, Elaine
saying,
- I've had enough,
but doing nothing beyond slamming a door or dropping a
plate.

One evening, when we were already in bed, I heard Laszlo
come home drunk. I knew the signs, the loud and irregular
footsteps, the dropped keys, the street echoes, mumbled
exclamations and ejaculations, the slur of his tongue, the
Elvis ah-ha and *I Don't Care If The Sun Don't Shine* sung out

of tune and off-key, and a loud and humble,
- Well, thank you, ma'am,
when he found his key, his voice sticking in his throat, sliding down his legs and into the gutters as he spoke. He kicked the milk bottles over, as he always did, and mumbled,
- Thank you, ma'am,
again as he put the key in the lock. And I whispered,
- Shut up, Laszlo,
to thin air, pulling the sheet over our heads, and wishing that I couldn't hear him, falling up the stairs as he climbed them.
- Elaine,
he shouted.
- Elaine.

And I wondered where she was, and fell asleep, and when I awoke I could hear Laszlo's voice murmuring through the floor, moments of silence followed by a harsh crescendo and a return to the rhythm. There was a crash and a door swung open, the voices suddenly louder.
- I've had enough,
Elaine was shouting,
- I'm going.
- Go then.
he said,
- I don't need this.

Her footsteps echoed down the stairs, and the front door slammed. We pulled the sheets over our heads and tried to sleep, woken by a knock on the window that we tried to ignore, a silence and then another. I crawled out of the bed and lifted the curtain, and saw Elaine outlined against the light of the streetlamps, imploring me, through the glass, to let her in, her forefinger touching her lips.

- Ah na,

I said, and Alice moaned and turned over on the bed, her legs at angles, the sheet dispersed towards the floor. I pulled a towel around my crotch, and tiptoed through the hall to let her in. She went straight into our room, shut the door and turned the key in the lock. Alice pulled the sheet across her body, and said,

- God, Elaine,

but she needn't have worried, for Elaine wasn't worried about us. She said to be quiet, please. She didn't want Laszlo to hear. He was crazy and she didn't understand him anymore. He was beyond reason, and all she wanted to do was sleep on our sofa, go upstairs in the morning and pack her things.

Why didn't he understand the simple things she wanted, how easy it would be for them to be happy if only he would try? I filled the kettle under the tap. I put the kettle onto the gas ring. I lit the flame with a match, and listened to the words, while Alice lay on her side, with her head cupped in her hand looking into Elaine's eyes, yawning.

- He's so clever,

Elaine said,

- but he doesn't know what to do with it. You are so unfair to Laszlo. You never give him a chance.

- But he isn't fair to you, is he?

said Alice, and she said,

- You don't like Elvis, do you?

as if that clinched the matter. We could hear him through the ceiling, his boots scraping the floor and the music filling the room above us – which wouldn't have mattered if he hadn't called her name at the top of his voice, which wouldn't have mattered either if she hadn't replied, and he hadn't come

running down – falling down – the stairs, shouting her name.
- Elaine.
And she swayed unsteadily against the door.
- Where are you?
- I'm here.
- Elaine.

She fell to the floor by the door, and we could see his shadow on the other side. Alice was looking at me, her eyes wide open and unbelieving. She was close to laughing. I smiled at her and put my finger to my lips. I still had nothing on but a towel around my hips.
- I don't believe this,
she said, and Laszlo heard her.
- Let her go,
he shouted, and I moved towards the door to let her out, but she stopped me. And Laszlo threw himself against the door, and it fell across her where she lay, leaving him standing there with an expression on his face of perfect violence. He would have hit me if my towel hadn't fallen away and left me naked in front of him. Alice swayed unsteadily on the bed with her sheet around her body, and said,
- Get out of my room,
And he lifted Elaine from under the door, pulled her arm across his shoulder, and carried her through the hall and up the stairs, limp on his shoulders with her head buried in his neck.

We hung a sheet across the doorway and went to bed, waking often through the hours of darkness, disturbed by a sound like bodies falling down the stairs.

The next morning we rose early. I went to the hardware

shop on the London Road, bought some hardboard and nails and hammered the door back together. We left the house and walked the streets until evening, coming home to the familiar smells of the hallway, of a century of cooked stew and floor polish, and found Laszlo and Elaine standing at the top of the stairs like a couple posing for a studio portrait, Elaine in a fifties' cotton frock, Laszlo in slacks and brothel-creepers, his hair rising off his head like surf.

Elaine grasped Laszlo's hand with her lean fingers and stiffened to face us. Laszlo's face and shoulders were stark and upright.

- We have to talk to you,

said Elaine.

- OK.

I fiddled with the key in the lock of our patched door. But she demanded a response.

- Can you look at me when I am talking to you?

- Ha.

Alice yawned and pulled open the door, disbelieving what she was hearing. I smiled at Elaine, her face crisp and firm like the folds of a daily newspaper. I flattened my hands along my jeans.

- Yes.

- I'm talking to you.

- Yes.

- We've been thinking about things.

She stared at the wall above my head, and I instinctively looked up at the picture-rail and the wallpaper there, looking for the focus of her vision.

- We like you very much, but we think that you should leave.

I didn't bother to answer, nodding and smiling with closed

lips.

- We tried, but it just didn't work,

she said.

- and we want you to leave.

I nodded again.

- Did you hear me?

- Yes.

- As soon as we can.

I said, and shut the door behind me on the picture of Laszlo and Elaine, the stilted English couple holding hands in the face of adversity. And in the following minutes the record-player came on upstairs, strangely restrained, a light colouring of noise trickling down through the ceiling, a plane rising through the evening sky with metal wings balanced on thin air and a row of Marmite jars climbing the tilting marble of their mantelpiece.

We left a few days later, packing our things into a rented Transit van, saying nothing to them, and went to the pub at the end of the street for a drink before we drove away. We walked hand in hand, swinging our arms like children, kicking the litter that lined the street as the sun fell through the clouds along the horizon, splintering on the roofs of the houses on the hill, exalted and relieved, when, from out of nowhere, Elaine ran up behind us.

- Ah na,

I said beneath my breath as she reached to grab Alice's elbow.

- Yes?

said Alice, but she didn't say anything. She opened her mouth to speak, but the words wouldn't come out. The street was empty and strangely silent, a silence that whirled around her

face. Alice tapped her on the arm, and said,
- Maybe we'll come and see you.
- No,
Elaine said.
- You won't.

Alice wiped the corner of her eye with the back of her hand, blinking involuntarily, and looked beyond Elaine. A man in a vest and trousers up to his armpits stood in a doorway.
- What are you lookin' at?
he said, and slammed the door behind him, leaving a sound that echoed down the street.

Richard Hillesley

Looking For God on the Mile End Road

When I was young the streetlights sang. The cold sun dipped in the river at six, cracked like an egg on the ships' hulls and house-ends, dripping white and yellow on split glass and wet slate. We ran a race to the lane's ending, slid in the gutters and sang.

Out in the street there was the smell of wet smoke, and we played football behind the coalsheds, whoosh, hack his legs from under him, running through the streets with the ball in the cold winds of February. We ran a race to the lane's ending, slid in the gutters and sang.

One evening, just before the sun went down, we were playing in the back lane when Mel Jamieson, trying for a header, jumped into the air and knocked the ball over the wall into Kowalski's back yard.

That was the first time we saw Kowalski. He had moved in during the previous spring. Mrs Paterson had told us about him: that he was odd, that he came and went during the night, and was gruff when she passed him in the street.
- He has a foreign accent,
she said, and that clinched it for us.

We stood to attention and knocked on his door but he didn't answer, so we pushed Mel into shinning over the wall. He stood on the dustbin, one foot in a crack between the bricks, one on the bin, and heaved himself up.
- Can yis see it?
someone said, and he said,
- Na,
poised there with his legs dangling in space.

- Haway,
someone said.

O'Brien, on the step opposite with his arms around his knees, flicked a piece of gravel into the air. Mel jumped and fell with a clang into the yard. He threw the ball over the wall, ran for the gate, and pulled back the bolt when Kowalski's hand landed on his neck.

We had never seen anything like it. Kowalski lifted Mel into the air and held him suspended, and, though I don't know why, we all burst out laughing. It was a nervous kind of laughter, for we were all balancing on our heels ready to scatter if he should move towards us. His big eyes flashed in the dusk. Mel dropped from his grip and ran on all-fours towards the end of the lane, and the rest of us stood our ground so as not to look soft in front of the others.

- A kna about yis lot,
Kowalski shuddered as his voice boomed out across the evening terraces.

- A kna about yis lot,
he said, in his hybrid accent of local vowels and foreign consonants.

- Whar'ave we done?
we said, and he said,

- Yi kna what yis have done,
and looked at us, one by one, with a long and silent stare.

- A haven't done owt.

- O yes,
he said,

- O yes,
and he looked at O'Brien and slowly lifted and pointed his finger,

- A have seen yis.

  And O'Brien shifted uncomfortably.
- Whar' am a supposed to 'ave done?
- Smokin',

he said,
- A have seen yis.
- Yis 'ave not.

  And he slowly shook his head.
- You can hide your evildoing from the world. You can hide it from yourself. But you cannot hide it from the Lord.
- A'm not evil,

said O'Brien, and Kowalski paused and glared at the tops of our heads.
- If you tell lies the Lord will bring damnation on you.
- A don't believe yis. A niver said me prayers, an' it niver harmed me.
- It will, me lad. It surely will, for the Lord will make me the instrument of your punishment.

  We were transfixed, and stood in silence while he looked around us and slowly backed away and shut the door behind him.
- Did yis hear that?

I had known O'Brien since I was so high. We grew up in the same street and went to the same school. He was the gawky kid with a ridge of hair that blew off his head and one of those faces that always got him into trouble. He looked like he had just done something terrible and he was pleased about it. I couldn't define what it was. It came somewhere between the freckles and the chin and the surprised look in his eyes that always made me laugh.

I was the innocent one who was led into trouble by O'Brien, but we knew it wasn't like that, that we led each other and he always got the blame. We rang old ladies' doorbells and ran like the wind when they shook their fists at the empty streets behind us. We threw fireworks into corner shop doorways and catapulted stones at lamp posts on school evenings just to watch the light shatter through the puddles. And we always got it in the neck at school.

That winter, we stole Kowalski's bicycle from outside his kitchen door, not for keeps, O'Brien said, but to see him angry. We knew how he would be. He would come looking for us with a blether and a strut, bow-legged and bow-shouldered, sprung like a taut arrow, zing, across the backlanes and washing lines. He would throw profanities in the air and stamp on the ground till the earth trembled and the stars flew around the sky. That was how it would be, but it didn't happen that way, for he had become our friend in a strange way.

He took us into his house and talked to us, myself and Mel and Jonah and O'Brien and Lorraine Gallagher and that friend of hers with the squint. We went up to his kitchen and sat round his table while he stood by the fireplace with his thumbs in his braces, and told us how it was.

We were kids and we didn't believe him, but it made no difference. His house was drab and thick and dreary, like an old man's house. We didn't go to learn anything. We went to taste the smell of churches, of fluff and Bibles, and to peer into his eyes, which were popping and unco-ordinated and thyroid-skewiff. When he looked at you, you were never sure whether he was looking into your eyes or beyond you into a crack in reality, for his gaze was lost in the silence that surrounded his thoughts. We may as well not have been there as the words he spoke took him higher and higher. He opened the dam and the words poured over us, fiery words full of grit and brimstone, words of light and truth directed at some mystical point between heaven and his kitchen door, words like Sodom and Gomorrah and the Whore of Babylon, who walked across our imaginations and into our hearts, words of hope and anger that poured into every crack of our beings, until he crumpled into a fragile silence, and the echo and the image of his words were left bouncing around the room, and he stood alone and suddenly vulnerable, a sad and lonely old man with a crust that was hard and brittle, and whose words kept his demons at bay.

He was mad, definitely mad, with a vision that pierced the opacity of outward forms but misread the core. He was mad with a belief the world could not live up to. He jammed his spectacles hard on his nose, sat stark upright at the table and opened his Bible with hands that were huge and clumsy, and read aloud chapter and verse from the Holy Bible, his voice echoing and booming like an organ-pipe in an empty cathedral.

The sun left a pool of light on the window, netting a cloud on the Sea of Galilee, and the Biblical rhythms flowed off his tongue like driving wheels, clattering down the line, taking off the rails and floating into space. And if we, who were only there to laugh at him, and to hear his strange and lying stories, should distract each other by talking or kicking or whispering, he would stop, and, with his head bent low, glare over the tops of his spectacles with a silence that spoke much louder than words. Those were the moments we loved. Innocently, squat on our haunches, we would ask him questions he could not answer.

- Mister Kowalski,

we would ask with big eyes,

- Do you know what God looks like?

And he would cough and glare, and shine his spectacles with the cloth from his pocket, searching for the words in the dark thick air.

- Has He a big beard?
- Don't hurry me, lad, don't hurry me.
- Is it as big as that?
- Where does he live?
- Does he tread on it?
- Is He fat?

And he would look uneasy, fiddling with his Bible and praying for inspiration from the pages that had blown cold through the centuries. He would stutter and hum, his thoughts abrupt and clipped and hesitant until he found his stride, and his voice banged and flew like the strokes of a mighty hammer on a magic anvil. Lies moulded truth in his big black heart, burning solid and heavy, and his words on fire melted objection, while we wallowed in the glow, eyes turned to the light until the sermon ended, or we tired of the loud voice and the intimidating silence and ran for the door.

We stole his bike one quiet evening after school. We had not meant to steal his bike. It just happened that way. We were nine or ten at the time and came down the lane with a surreptitious cigarette, half expecting a harangue from the old man who was always looking out of his window to witness the irreligion of his neighbours, but he wasn't there, and we sat on his step, passing the ciggie between us. His bike leant against the kitchen door, with a rusting frame and missing spokes.

O'Brien knocked on the window and had no answer. I sat on the bike with one foot on the ground so as to keep my balance. I wasn't thinking of stealing it, but it seemed natural to ride it round the yard through the puddles even though I couldn't reach to put my bum on the saddle. I skated round with one foot on the pedals and one foot on the ground, and O'Brien shouted up at the window, but Kowalski didn't come. So we rode it into the lane and skidded round through the puddles, whooping and shouting, wheee.

O'Brien hung on the back with his legs in the wind, and I pedalled like a madman, hoying it down the hill past houses in clouds of smoke, evening lampposts and elder brothers off to the club in corduroy ties and shrunken suits. We rode for miles and miles and the basket and saddle clattered as we swung in the mud through the goalposts on the park by the dirt-tip and the cloudfilled sky. A coppa saw us, and waved an angry hand, to be on with it home to our mams in the withering light. And we jumped off and pushed it ower the road.

- Does he kna it's stolen?
- It's not stolen. We borra'd it.
- A kna that, but does he kna that?
- He's gone, hasn't he?
- Scab.
- Gerron wit.

The sun sank in the sulphur over our shoulders, bruising the sky above the shadows of houses and the pit. I pushed the bike along the road and O'Brien walked behind me with his hands in his pockets. He wandered off onto the grass kicking a can he had found, and lay down with his hands behind his head. I put the bike down where it was, half on the road, half on the pavement, and stood there.

- Yis got a tab?

I said, and he pulled out a Number 6 packet with a dumper inside it. He nicked them from his mam's bag. I used to watch him doing it. He would be talking to her, playing the sweet child while he ransacked her bag though he was careful and never took more than a few pence and a tab. The tab was a ritual we had between us. I would light it and blow the smoke around my face. I never inhaled and I never coughed. He always inhaled and posed which was something I never understood, but I never laughed because that was part of the ritual, the understanding we had that we were doing something that was forbidden and therefore special.

And while we were lying there on the grass, blowing smoke into the air, a car came by, running across the wheels of the bike where it lay half on the grass and half on the road, and we jumped up and shouted at him, but he was gone and we knew that we had no-one to blame but ourselves.

- Bastad,

O'Brien kept saying, but I knew and knelt over the remains of the bike.

- It's broke,

I said.

- Bastad,

he said.

- What'll we do?

The spokes and the back wheel were twisted out of shape. We dragged it behind us and it reproved us with its presence.

43

At Harton Dyeworks pond, blue-green light on the water, scum on the ditch. The trees had begun to screech as the icy wind mopped up the leaves. Everything was slowly dribbling outwards. We stood against the railings, the bike held in our hands with effort, balanced on top. I said,
- Shall wis push it in?
- Dare yis.

I don't think we meant it, but we turned and smiled as the sludge opened and the water bubbled. A few stray weeds tangled in the spokes. We stayed, hanging on the railings, until the water went still, leaving a dark stain on the surface, and turned and went home.

The bicycle stayed with me. It had a life and a ghost of its own, and I dreamt about it, rising out of the Harton Dyeworks pond and following me home, its ghostly wheels spinning through my dreams. Two or three nights later we were back outside Kowalski's place, playing the usual game of shouting up at his window and asking to be let in. We listened for him but he did not answer, and my heart was not in it.

A damp light glowed in his window and the wind blethered through the wires, and I dragged O'Brien with me through the unlocked door and up the creeping stairs to Kowalski's room, where he sat in the cold on his hard chair in his coat, as sad and ambiguous as the black Bible that slept on his side table.
- A niver done owt,
he said.
- Wha's the marra?
- Me bike's bin stole,
Kowalski said, and stared before his eyes into the empty

fireplace without a fire, not looking at us, and we pushed each other back out through the door.

We went to the Harton Dyeworks pond. We did not talk all the way but we knew it was a matter of pride and urgency. We climbed over the railings and hung on, dredging with a stick until we found the bike. O'Brien stood up to his knees in the slurry and muck, as we pulled at the tangle and heaved and pulled the bicycle onto the pavement. There was not much of it. Weeds and muck tangled in the spokes and chain but we pushed it all the way home, wet and cold and shivering and unhappy, and leant it against the wall where we had found it.

- It's useless,

I said, and O'Brien said,

- Bastad.

Richard Hillesley

Words And Birds

School was terrible. Rising in the morning, walking up the lane, first words frosted in air. The bare trees were stark and still. I waited for the break times to play soccer in the yard with bottletops or tennis balls and share a tab behind the sheds. And the days were lost in oblivion, leaning on a bent desk, while the teacher's voice scratched across the silence, punctuated by shuffles and whispers and stifled laughs from the back row. And the best teacher I had was not tough or methodical. He was a simple man who loved his subject, which was English Literature, and strode the corridors of the school with his legs bowed at the knees and his face torn across with poetic speculation.

- Poetry, lads,

he would announce, standing by the board, rubbing his hands together, and he would dive bird-like into the lesson, his cultured accent stumbling and sliding into a North-umbrian strut as he recited into the sky of the class.

- Mavluss, lads, mavluss,

he would say in between lines, his brow leaning on the clouds, forgetting about us kids altogether. He may as well have been high above Derwentwater reading to sheep. He cupped his hands and mimicked the calls of peewits and curlews and kittiwakes to illustrate onomatopoeia and read poems the more loudly to emphasise intimations of immortality.

- Immaculate,

he would say in between lines. And we listened.

Once, when he was in mid-recital, another teacher knocked on the door, and he, not listening, held the book by his side, preferring to read from the heart, and continued. A head appeared around the door with a disconcerted smile and a misplaced air of confidence, and said,

- Excuse me, Mister Holden ...

But there was no hesitation and the rhythmic words broke and shook on the silence like a strong sea on solid rocks, or a storm crashing over Walla Crag or Skidaw.

- May I ... ?

the teacher said and Holden threw the book on the floor, the pages flying open, turned to the window and stared into his rage, refusing to answer, the dulled atmosphere hanging on a cliff-edge of silence until the other left.

And that was why we liked him, because he cared and was a natural. His thoughts were centred on the moment, being known to have skipped school when an oil-streak hit the beaches so he could care for the birds that had been washed ashore, flightless but alive.

- Terrible,

he would say, raging at the thoughtlessness of those who had forgotten the consequences of their actions.

He was oblivious to what we thought. He wasn't conscious of anything but the words and birds that moved him and the remarkable quality of being alive. He lived everything he taught us and we cared to work for him, knowing he would put aside a good essay and say,

- Mavluss, lad. Mavluss,

and your horizons would extend endlessly. But all that ended for me when I became his daughter's boyfriend in the sixth form and my marks descended mysteriously.

I had no idea who she was. It was a Saturday in October. A

cold sun hung over the church. Trees scratched marks along the skyline. Clouds in black and white. I saw her coming through a sea of faces in the market at three in the afternoon. Traders wrapped in steep coats against the damp. We were leaning against a wall in our sharp shoes and I saw her with her bright eyes and warm face. It was the year of the miners' strike, and everything was flat blue or grey. She caught my eye because she looked alive and in touch with reality, a quality I did not have.

Mel was doing his thing with his jug ears and the gaps in his teeth as she walked by, and asked,
- Do you believe in God?
and I said,
- Why?

I wished I hadn't, because he went off on one about his mam and the time she dragged him and his sister Alice to church when they were kids. Alice was five and spooked by the body on the cross and the smell of the priest in a frock. She looked up at her mam and tugged her dress and said,
- Mam. He's like a witch doctor.
- Shush.
- But, Mam, he is.
- Shush.
- But, Mam, he's like a witch doctor.

And the priest gave his flock a taste of the flesh and a sip of the wine.
- Body of Christ, Amen. Body of Christ, Amen.

And Alice spat on the floor and Mel couldn't stop laughing. So his mam took him outside and thumped him, and he never went to church again.
- And that is what a mean,

he said.

- If there is a God he's nuts, making a world like this and leaving it to itself, like starting a train and jumping off it before it starts moving.

But I wasn't listening. I was looking at her and she was looking at me. The black and lamplit air around my face. The lights in the buses in the middle of the day. She walked past me, and I followed but I didn't know what to say. I wanted to know her and said,

- Hi,

and she smiled. The sky clashed above us. A train rumbled over the Bridges, and she was gone.

- She's not for you,

Mel said.

- Why not?

I said.

That autumn and winter I saw her everywhere. Not that I was looking, but she was always there. I asked Yvonne who she was, and she told me.

- She's really nice,

she said,

- but there's no way she'll go out with you.

- Why not?

- She just won't.

Her name was Jane and she was a teacher's daughter and I was nothing, and I wasn't helping myself. In the winter I walked on ice. My mind was a fog adrift in the streets. Everything had its word and its rhythm. That was all I knew. Beneath me there was a void without a vision or an end, and she looked to me like she had none of that. That was what I saw in her. Someone whose certainties and worldliness might rub off on me.

I was always in trouble at school, and I was always late. I didn't like morning assembly or the smell in the hall of wood and polish and wet dufflecoats, and the coughing and scraping as the kid with the high voice read the lesson under the echoing roof of the school hall, or the headmaster read the names of kids who were on report for getting caught, for smoking or cursing and worse. Or the hymns we talked through while pretending to sing.

- A was with Jennifer Skipton last night,

we would sing.

- Yi wasn't.
- A was.
- Well?
- A dinnat believe yis. Did she?
- As if I'd tell yis.

We lost our virginity, or said we did, in the back streets after school, some at the age of eleven, some never, and we never really knew if the stories we told each other were true or not. It wasn't until years later we realised the kids we envied because they pulled the girls were doing day jobs and pushing prams, having missed out on the rest of their lives.

I saw her everywhere, and everywhere I saw her she caught my eye. She'd be looking and so would I. But we were too shy or vain to break the ice. Attraction put the fear in us of failure or rejection, or the fear that the image will not be equal to the reality and the image has become the thing itself, so we kept our distance, walking on ice so as not to tread on our dreams. I wondered if we would ever break the spell.

Winter was upon us and frost was on the ground. The strike was touching everything and nothing was right with the world. It seemed like we'd never talk to each other, until one Saturday evening when the sky was falling and the clouds were dark, and I was coming home from town and ran for a bus, and she was on the bus and I sat beside her.

We were shy and talked and I looked for a response, a smile behind her eyes or the brush of her hand against mine. We laughed and talked and the ice was broken. I said I would walk her home but we walked for miles, and sat on a bench and stared out to sea, shivering against the cold. After I left her I walked home with a bounce in my step, despite the frost on the ground.

We quickly became inseparable. I would meet her after school at the gates, waiting on the other side of the road.
- Why do you always stand on your own?
she said,
- I like to,
I said, and she told me I was strange. But it really wasn't so. It was a gesture, to give me separation from the crowd and a feeling of difference I really didn't have. We walked the streets, her in her school uniform, and me alive with the energy I borrowed from her.

We didn't kiss until a week after I had known her, one night in the cemetery when the night was already on top of us. We were desperate and clumsy, as if the sky had opened and angels had come down like birds to peck our skin, and this was the end of the world and the people of the town were rising to heaven between the Town Hall clock and the gas holder. We squeezed the air from each other's bodies.

51

Richard Hillesley

- I can't breathe,
she said, and we reached out to feel the mystery of our touch,
reeling under the stars and the streetlights revolving around
the sky, and felt something more real than we imagined.

I liked her because she was new and alive, and she brought
an innocence into my world. In the middle of winter we had
a spring in our step and were alive to our senses, adrift in our
otherworldliness. We hadn't felt like this before, and as far as
we could tell, nor had anyone else.

And if the world around us was mad and bad we weren't
oblivious to its iniquities. Some evenings we went down to
the Bridges and stood in the picket line at the gates of the
colliery. Even as kids we had no illusions. We knew what the
strike was about and we knew it would change our lives
forever.

One day I stole off school to meet her in the back lane by
the allotments. She leant against a wall, and threw her bag
over her shoulder when she saw me like she didn't have a
care, and we walked casually along the lane, touching lightly
as we walked.

We slipped into her parents' house, cold and heavy with
the smell of books, faded carpets climbing the stairs to the
stained glass window on the landing as she pulled me
towards her room, into a world that belonged to her alone,
smells that were new to me and a chill wind that blew in
through the curtains over her bed.

She sat on the bed, mattress and bedding collapsed in the
middle to fold a body into sleep. She rested her head on her
elbow, and I moved between fear and wonder, afraid to move
in case the atmosphere was disturbed, the cold sheets against
our bodies, the light falling across our faces, a bubble floating

in the air between us, drifting up from the pillow and alighting on our hair and skin. I was afraid it might burst and the spell of our knowing each other might turn to air.

It rained outside, a soft rain through the leaves of the trees in the yard, and we lay on top of the sheets, knowing ourselves yet disappointed too, hoping for more of the same yet uncertain of the limits of our desires, continuing the search for excitement in our nerve-ends and in the tips of our fingers, knowing that behind every pleasure we stole there was an underlying sadness, that the memory of touch dissolves and the memory moves on. Ecstasy is temporary and reality returns.

We were lying on the bed when there was a sudden bang and her dad came in through the front door. She was calm but I wasn't.

- Jane,

he called,

- ... you home?

She pulled her blouse around her, stood in her skirt on the floor, and tugged it up over her hips.

- Get under the bed,

she whispered. I crawled under the bed and she threw my clothes in behind me.

- Coming,

she shouted to him, pushing my shoes under the cover with her upside-down face next to mine,

- Shush,

she said with a finger to her lips and left me under the bed arching to pull on my trousers and shirt, struggling with the legs and sleeves. I listened to the radio and the voices coming through the floor, and heard the bang of a door and feet coming up the stairs. She pushed her face under the bed and pulled me out.

- Hurry,

she said, and I crawled into the light, tugging on my shoes, pushing my shirt into my trousers, stuffing my tie into a pocket, doing up my flies. I followed her down the stairs, trying to be quiet, hearing the creak of the wood loud on the stairs.

- Hurry,

she whispered. And I made it through the hall and into the rain in the street, still doing up my buttons, looking back to see her looking at me, waving as I walked up the street with rain in my hair and my shirt-tail sticking through my flies.

That night I lay in my bed and glowed like a comet scurrying along the fringes of the heavens, catapulted by gravity through the curving parabola of my dreams, a new discoverer of other worlds and distant planets.

A few days later she invited me home for tea.

- Na,

I said. I didn't want to meet her dad in his house. I really didn't.

I could see he wasn't pleased. I wore an uncomfortable tie and he smiled a teacher's smile as he stood to shake my hand. I stood among the smell of pipesmoke and fluff and didn't know where to put my hands. I ran my fingers from pockets to chin, through my hair and back behind my back, and tried to smile and appear relaxed while her mother said nice things to me. But it was difficult.

Her younger brother thought it was a laugh and watched me with a snigger playing around his lips. I knew his face. I had seen him once, in the cornershop, send the old lady up the ladder to the top shelf at the back of the shop to fetch a jar of humbugs so that he could fill his pockets with sweets from the counter while she wasn't looking.

- These?

she kept saying, halfway up the ladder, leaning awkwardly across the shelves.

- Na, those.

- Where?

she said.

- Left a bit. Ah na, I meant right. Those. Aye.

She came down the ladder, inelegant and ungainly, with a great glass jar of humbugs balanced in her plump hands, clutched to her breast, laid it on the counter and smiled. He said,

- Na, I didn't mean those,

and left without buying a thing, his pockets overflowing with a random selection from the counter.

He made it through the door and ran. Knowing I had seen him do this gave me some comfort, because though he was younger than Jane he used his age to bully her.

- I've seen you in the sweet shop, haven't I?

I said, in a moment when his dad was out of the room.

- so what?

he said.

- Nicking sweets,

I said. He sniggered less after that.

Holden didn't say much during the meal. He looked out the window a lot, absorbed by the dark clouds that slumped along the sky as if they were symbols of our mutual fate. It was an uncomfortable meal, and at the end he rose and left the room without a word. I felt the dark music of the leaves in the road, the rain splattering against the glass, the headlights of cars through the halflight of evening, and felt strangely alone though Jane sat beside me.

- He likes you really,

she said,

- He just finds it a bit difficult. He's not very good at these things.

Still he tried to give me space. Once or twice he took us into the Cheviots in his car, and he tried to make it work. He knew the places to see the birds, to feel the wind on our faces. He drove with his binoculars around his neck and suddenly pulled up, braking and shushing as he stopped to point at a kestrel hovering over the moor, swooping onto a spot in the mist and the grass.

- Mavluss,

he said, seeing some poetry in the movement, and we were caught in the excitement of the moment and the birds as he saw them, and we had to follow him over the walls and up the fells, looking for birds or signs of nature. And once or twice he grabbed me, put his binoculars into my hand, and said,

- Look at that,

pointing at a bird spinning over the horizon or a nest buried in the ground. And for that moment I felt included and accepted, and even a kind of intimacy.

Sometime near the end of February, I went with Jane down to the Bridges one evening to join the picket line. The sun glowed over the houses like the embers of a smouldering slag heap. The evening was quiet at first, smoke and warmth from the fire the pickets had lit by the colliery gate. But it didn't end that way. We were leaning against the railings on the other side of the road when the cops arrived. They weren't local and they had come in vans. Later they brought horses and set up roadblocks so nobody could get in or out.

They went in among the pickets waving batons and dragged people out of the line. A cop pulled a woman across the pavement by her hair and Jane jumped on his back and screamed at him. I tried to pull her away but the cops took her, kicking and screaming, into a police van.

I didn't know what to do, so I raced along the wall to the back gate into the coalyard, ripping my jeans as I scaled the gate, ran between the sidings and escaped over the back wall into the lane, twisting my ankle as I fell. I limped and ran all the way to the police station, just in time to see her dragged through the station to a police cell, when she screamed at me to get her dad. I called him from a phone box in the street, and told him Jane had been arrested.
- Where?
he said,
- On the picket line,
I said.
- What was she doing there?
- We were on the picket line.
- Why?
- The strike.
- Why?
- The police attacked the pickets.
- Why was she arrested?
- She jumped on a policeman.

- Why didn't you stop her?
- I tried.

The phone went dead. He arrived ten minutes later, walked up to me on the steps of the police station and said,
- You're never to see my daughter again.

I tried to tell him it wasn't my fault and I had tried to stop her, but he wasn't listening. Later I told Mel and he said,
- It's like the strike. You can give up or run away, or you can stick together and fight.

We decided to fight. She went to court but it could have been worse. She was charged with obstructing a police officer in the course of his duty and was warned to stay out of trouble. We kept on seeing each other but decided to give him time and stay out of sight. All went well until a Saturday afternoon two or three weeks later when we sat in the cafe in the market place with onions and saveloys and gravy slithering down our fingers, and she said to me,
- I have to stop seeing you,

I wasn't sure whether she meant to say what she was saying or was looking for a response from me. Across the street the bells in the church were ringing. There was a wedding going on, and the instruments and bones of marriage and prayer were jangling in the breeze. I said,
- Why?
- Because ...
- I thought you said you liked me,
I said.
- I do.
- Why?
- You'll never amount to anything,

she said, licking her fingers with her legs crossed, inspecting the tips of her fingers for spots of gravy, flicking a piece of onion off the corner of her skirt, not looking at me. I didn't know what I was supposed to say.

- I haven't even started yet,
I said.
- I know.
- Well?
- You'll never have any money,
she said.
- You don't know that, and, anyway, I don't want any money.
- You do.
- Not like that, I don't. And anyway. You always said you didn't care about stuff like that.

She didn't say anything.

- It's your dad, isn't it?
I said, and she avoided my eyes and looked out the window.
- If that's what you think,
I said, and walked away, thinking that she would follow me, but she didn't.

I didn't go out for days. I lay on my bed and stared at the ceiling. The strike was over and lost. Spring was dragging its heels and I was missing her. One night Mel came round. He was bored and wanted to go to the club. I went to please him and stood in a corner, hiding in the music and the lights and the smoke. I hadn't meant to see her but bumped into her as she came out of the toilets. She was as surprised as I was, and was as shy and nervous of me as I was of her.

- Please,
she said,
- Don't ignore me.

59

- I wasn't ignoring you,
I said.
- You were,
she said,
- Why did you finish with me?
- I didn't,
I said.
- You did. You walked away from me when I was talking to you.

The band began to play, loud and mediocre, and she brushed my face with her hair, put her lips to my ear and said,
- You didn't ring me.
- What?
- You didn't ring me,
she shouted.
- I couldn't,
I said.
- I know.

She stood beside me, playing self-consciously with her hands.
- It's too hot in here,
she said,
- Shall we go outside?
- I suppose so,
I said, and we stood outside with the light splintering over our shoulders and the shivers climbing up our backs. A train rolled over the Bridges, shaking the buildings, clacking and roaring along the hinges of my spine, and we left with our arms around each other, floating on the warmth of our breath.

For a while, at least, we were back together, but school

became more difficult. Holden would not forgive me for my sins. He ignored me, looking over my head if I put my hand up in class.

- Not you,

he would say, with a dismissive gesture of his hand. Not that I cared. But it didn't make me feel good. I felt like the people he had warned us against, the Philistines and the pilferers of birds' eggs.

- A lazy piece of work,

he wrote on one of my essays, and I avoided his eyes as he avoided mine, though I caught him once peering at me over the tops of his spectacles with narrowed eyes. I waited until the classroom had cleared and said,

- Sir.

- Yes.

- What's wrong with it?

He shook his head, grim lips and furrowed eyebrows, and turned to wipe the board clean. I was unable to move, rooted to the ground.

- You know,

he said.

- But I really worked on that,

I said. He stared out the window and didn't answer me.

- You know what the problem is,

he said, and folded his books under his arm and walked towards the door and left me there, staring at the board.

- But that's not fair,

I said to his shadow, picked up my exercise book and threw it across the floor. He peered at me sternly, unsmiling, and said,

- You shouldn't have done that.

61

But what else could I have done? I couldn't say anything, picked up my bag and walked past him and out of the school.

On the Lea with Jane, high over the cliffs. The sea and the sky were unforgiving and unrepentant. We sat on a cold bench, looking out to sea, hands in pockets, tugged by the wind, like birds with a long journey before us, and no let up. The wind slipped its fingers inside our shirts, and I stared with cold eyes into my future. She said,
- What are you trying to say?
and I couldn't find the words I felt comfortable saying, so I said what I didn't want to say.
- I want to finish it,
I said.
- Why?
- I just think we should.
I said, and because I wanted to sound like I meant it I said,
- I don't like you anymore.
She stared out to sea, shuddering, and I felt nothing at all. I was elated for I had done something terrible. It wasn't until I was on my way home that it hit me, a dryness in my throat, my coat pulled around me. I banged my head against the window like a drunk on the last bus and felt suddenly hurt and empty, but it was too late by then.
When I got home my mother said,
- Where have you been?
and I shrugged my shoulders.
- It's time you got your act together,
she said, and I sat at the kitchen table with the tea she had poured me, blew the steam from the rim of the cup, thumbed my lip, and wished I was somewhere else.

Unbanging The Nails

'The water is wide and I cannot cross over
Nor do I have wings to fly
Build me a boat that could carry two
And both shall row, my love and I'

This country has history in its bones, washed down by the streams of ancient water, through the rocks and pebbles, echoes of sound and rhythm in the stone. The sun falls through the clouds, moving pools of light and shade across the valleys. In a break between the clouds is a pub, a stone house with a low wall, a car park, and three trees. The highest pub in Wales, though one of several that make that claim, sat in a shaft of light between the gorsefalling peaks.

Ben had come early one summer in a Morris Minor. He camped on the farmer's land up the valley in a flat blue tent. I met him in the pub, a big man with a red face and big hands, thumbs hooked into the leather belt that struggled to hold up his trousers. He stood at the end of the bar, whisky in one hand and a pipe in the other, and spoke through a long beard with a rasping voice that sometimes broke into loud laughter.

When it was your turn to speak he would twist his head to one side and look at you oddly, his mouth puckered and his eyebrows raised as if to say,
- Is that so?
as he waited for a pause to dive into, to separate you from your thoughts. He looked at you, his eyes screwed up and his head shaking though his body was still, and he would say,
- Interesting,

63

like a full-stop. He twisted his jaw and the words came out, considered and slow, demanding attention. His head would lift and his voice got louder, and you listened to what he had to say. He had been everywhere and he had done everything. He had been a teacher of mathematics, and he had been to Africa and Asia. He had been up the Orinoco in search of El Dorado in the footsteps of Gonzalo Pizarro and Wolf and Francisco de Orellana who, as they starved and died on the banks of the Rio Coca, wrote,

- After boiling our boots in herbs we set off for the kingdom of gold.

As if life were that simple. And didn't we know it, who had tried to make our way through life with the simplest of jobs, to earn a crust and find some pleasure on the side, and had found the world displeased by our desires. Ben had no simple ideas. He was going to change the world, to make a hero of himself. He painted, though I never saw his paintings. He wrote poetry, though I never read a word he wrote. And he talked about what he was going to do though I saw him do very little.

For him, it seemed, the idea and the ambition were enough. Truth followed in their wake, illuminating the shadows. And if that were not enough, he would have another idea. It didn't seem to matter that he hadn't done the things he told us. The physical truth was unimportant. What mattered was that he had transported himself into a parallel universe where everything he told us was true. And if it wasn't true, it should have been.

I don't know where he came from. It hardly mattered. But it wasn't hard to imagine the northern streets in the northern rain, where he walked the narrow pavements to a provincial job in a provincial town, where everybody knew the ins and outs of his life, where his mother and father watched him from their door, and watched him coming home again, where every girlfriend had known him all his life and his imagination was filtered through the smoke and bricks of his back street and the local recreation ground.

He would tell you how coming to this place had set him free and we knew that it was true. When he came here nobody knew or cared who he was or where he came from. He came into this world with new experiences and a fresh vision. And people wanted to hear and believe the stories he told. And the stories spread and grew like the rhododendrons that had taken root in the valley, clinging for life to the outcrops and landfalls. The weeds of his imagination sprouted bright flowers but strangled the native roots. That is what I said when I was asked. But they preferred his untruth to my reality.

After a month or two he found a cottage up the valley that had no electricity or running water.
- Just the thing,
he said, in that way of his. Up at the crack of dawn, doing sit-ups in the fields and running on the spot, gulping the mountain air that blew straight down the valleys, glowing as he walked up the hill with a bucket and washed himself in the clear water from the spring.

At night a paraffin lamp and a log fire lit the cottage, and he would come down from the hills to the pub, put his pipe in his mouth and drink, walking all the way with that proud gait of his, chest out, thumping the air.

One night that winter, Ben came into the pub from the

snow, stamping his boots and blowing into his hands, braced by the wind that ripped up the valley, and told me, hard against the fire, that he was going to build a boat in the yard of the pub, a replica of an early medieval ship, that he would sail across the Atlantic to prove that the Welsh discovered America. The notion was absurd to me, that he could build a boat on his own, in the yard of the pub, that would cross the ocean. I didn't believe a word of it, nor that the Welsh had discovered America. I was too lazy and impractical for such dreams, and believed the same of him. I thought he would talk through his obsession, spit it out and move on after a while, but I was wrong.

Within weeks, he had moved into a caravan in the yard and a sign went up on the wall of the pub, on which was written: - The Welsh discovered America, next to the cutting from the Liverpool Evening Echo about the black slave in the seventeen-hundreds who married the daughter of a farmer in the valley and had seven children called Jones.

The caravan was ancient, a fifties' Bluebird or Sprite rescued from a yard in Aberystwyth, shaped like a bubble and thick with the smell of fifties' holidays on the coast of Wales, fish and chips and quarrels on rain-spoiled days, thin curtains faded by the light of the sun, cushions that had memories stained into their threads, sat in the gravel of the yard of the pub against a low drystone wall.

Beyond was a stream, sliding between stones and clumps of grass. The wind played a sad and insistent music through the rocks and grass, the wires and the signs that knocked and whirred the whole night long. The stone pub was defiant, an outpost in a land of gorse and fern and stubbled grass, the wind ripping through gaps in the mountains, the water slithering down through the rocks and stubborn moss.

Ben would emerge at morning from the door of his caravan, yawning and stretching, his breath rising in shapes through the air, his shirt streaked with dirt, hitch up the belt that held up his trousers, wash his face under the tap in the yard, and set to work on constructing his dream from the shadows of his bills and debts. Out of hope a little came of tangible reality, a cleared space in the yard, wood donated by a builder's yard in the local village, second hand tarpaulins and ropes from a chandler in town.

And we would marvel at the wonder of what he was doing, the bits of his boat heaped up and taking shape in this yard in the clouds against a backdrop of hills that were harsh and steep, bending into the soft green of the fields below, the mist and predictable rain, the sea moss and silt of the estuary, the birds rising through the half light below. He begged for money and materials from sponsors and charities and local businessmen. To beg with success is to keep your pride, to prise the morsels out of closed pockets with dignity, and Ben begged with pride and dignity. He gathered his bits and pieces as he needed them, through the gift of the gab and a sense of mission that overturned doubt, and this made him as strong as he needed to be during those early months when the outline of the boat rose from the gravel in the yard, a thing of beauty and wonder.

We marvelled at the beauty of his dream, however pompous or irrational it might have been. And we were proud that he had built his boat in the yard of our pub, and would have loved him just as much for his failure as his success. The dream is what really matters in this life, not the substance, for the dream colours and informs the reality, and without the dream there are only cold forms and shadows to walk between.

He was sailing in the wake of the Welsh Prince Madoc who had discovered America in 1170, a fact that Ben told us was indisputably true. He had a photograph of a plaque that the Daughters of the Revolution had erected near Mobile, Alabama, in memory of Madoc's landing there. His followers from the Mawddach and Drwywd estuaries had become the Welsh Indians of North America, building mounds and forts along the length of the Mississippi and Missouri rivers as they migrated westwards.

He told us that this was true, and that in the eighteenth century a Welsh missionary called John Evans travelled into the wilderness at the headwaters of the Missouri and found the descendants of Madoc among the Mandan Indians, who welcomed him as a brother and spoke to him in Welsh. The Mandans died out after the coming of the white man, as a result of war and disease, and the myth of Madoc and the Welsh Indians survives in dreams and the heart from Penrhyndeudraeth to Patagonia.

History says that the myth was a creation of the alchemist John Dee to counter the Spanish claim to have discovered America, but history to Ben was just a different dream.

By the time the girl arrived, during the first summer, the boat had a skeleton and bones, ribs and a keel, and the yard was stacked with piles of materials and provisions, tethered under tarpaulins. It was a bright summer, patches of light and shadow moving over the land, the clouds rolling across the pieced and plotted fields of the valley, soft wind stroking up the slopes from the valley floor.

She came from out of the blue, from the Americas, a descendant of the Navajos of the south-west, with high cheekbones and warm dark eyes. The name she came with was Caroline but we called her Cochise. I didn't know how she came to be there, or where she had met Ben.

I first met her with him in the pub, and she had already fallen under his spell and walked into his dreams, innocent and alive, and touched his soul. She had moved from a tent on the hillside and into Ben's caravan, and sat at his side in the pub while he pronounced and elucidated, evoked and provoked and shaped the world in his image, absorbed in his world, and yet somehow apart. She exuded an air of distance and calm, like some bird that glided above, bemused and amused by the world below. She looked on him with a kindly understanding, as if her mission were to guide him away from himself and towards a better self.

Yet there was something in him that she yearned for, that she couldn't master or touch, that gave her an imperceptible strength when she was with him, a weakness in him that made her strong. She needed to be with him, to put his ship on a stable course and to be his guiding star, to cross the wild oceans with him, to risk her life, tossed and bucketed and thrown, rolled and pitchpoled and overwhelmed, at the mercy of the elements in his impossible ark on its mythic voyage across the sea to discover America.

They would be like the vagrants and the vagabonds of history who left the shores of Europe in search of the miraculous, the pilot of the Pinta, Magellan or Amerigo Vespucci, men who dared to dream, who sailed over the rim of the world and fell into the unknown with only their dreams for sustenance and the stars to follow, and brought in their wake the gold-diggers and the Godfearing and the restless. As if Cochise had a need to discover the secrets of her own land beyond the charted seas and the terrible dream of history. Sailing the ocean for her would be to come to a better understanding of herself.

Ben was making a new world for himself from the materials of the old, the myths and the trees and the wind of Wales. He sat in the pub with his beard wagging, Cochise at his side, giving him a strength that drew on the dark centre of his world, and his image and his powers increased like the boat in the yard, like the winds that blew across the mountains twisting the trees out of shape, the fire in the pub popping and flaring, rising and falling beneath his gaze, his beer wetting the rhythm of his speech.

And I feared for him, the lost boy inside him that I knew was afraid of the dark, frightened of the wild ocean, of the disturbing sea, with its hidden depths and mythic monsters, irascible tempers and cold deceits, afraid for the safety of his boat of dreams, afraid that Cochise would see him for what he was, that he only wanted to dream, afraid that he would lose her if she knew the truth, a truth that she already knew, that his fear reached to the bottom of his soul, though none of us cared if he never left us, if he never sailed his boat away. We didn't care if he stayed in the pub until his hundredth year, entertaining us with his dreams, but we couldn't tell him, for to tell him would be to destroy the illusion that sustained him, and stirred us to like him in the first place.

We scorned Ben and we admired him because of the audacity of his dreams, because the dreams had taken shape in the yard of our pub, where we could see them when we stumbled out to the toilets for a piss, a hulk of wood and skin, a boat to cross the ocean, something to show off to the tourists who looked us over, the Captain in the corner of the pub with his Indian handmaiden and his books and maps on the table beside him.

Ben's weakness to us was his strength. We liked him for being a failure, for the goals he failed to score as much as those he did. To us he was the John Charles or Ryan Giggs of our valley, far from the reach of the outside world, and we welcomed him for daring to dream, for being the one to turn against the crowd with his feet in the air, and for his sudden anger when someone questioned his dreams.

- And what have you done?

he would say.

- How dare you criticise me?

Like when Cedric Jones asked him if it hadn't been done before, hadn't someone sailed a skin boat across the North Atlantic via the Faroes and Iceland to the rim of the Arctic Ocean to prove that the Irish Papas had been there first, and anyway hadn't the Vikings gone to Newfoundland by the year a thousand? Ben stood up, rigid in his braces, his beard pointing towards the door like a compass or a sundial, slammed his glass on the table, and blew out of the room in a silent rage. He stood in the yard, indignant and proud, his arms across his chest, looking into the distant recesses of the clouds and his heart. And Cedric, bemused and bewildered, followed him out there, put his hand on his shoulder, and said,

- I'm sorry, Ben.

Ben held his jaw up, proud to the hills, and said nothing. Cedric said,

- I didn't mean to hurt you, Ben,

Silence followed, but for the drip of water into the drains, flush of an emptied sink, a slow wind through the night, and Ben held his chin upturned, lips pursed, the fingers of his right hand teasing out his beard, and he said,
- You didn't hurt me,
and went back inside, as if nothing had happened.

'There is a ship and she sails the seas
She's burdened deep as deep can be
But not as deep as the love I'm in
And I know not if I sink or swim'

The boat grew through that first summer and the following winter, like a tree bursting through the rocks and gravel of the yard, the ribs and the torso, the tarpaulins over the top, a living thing of sap and leaves and roots, and these seemed like idyllic times that we lived in, when all was right with the world. There was a peace over the yard, the boat, and the rocking caravan between the stones.

Cochise brought with her a restlessness in the face of nature and its temperaments that she knew and recognised. It was her quiet will that forced the boat to materialise. Where Ben might have sat back and rested on his hands, Cochise forced the issue, put tools into his hands, drove him down the valley in the ancient Morris to bring back the crucial implements for his desires, pushed him into realising his dream, for his own sake and for hers. She had resources of spirit where he had none. She had a courage and determination that he lacked. She had the resilience and the wish to struggle against the odds and wild and unforgiving sea, where he would lie back and dream. She blew life into his dreams. They worked in the yard, nailing and sawing and hammering, caulking the planks, sometimes helped by a young carpenter from the town, who strutted like a cock, baseball cap at angles through the yard, and chided them for their efforts, showing off to the girls in anoraks and climbing boots who stopped at the pub on summer days, a cigarette between his lips, his chest and shoulders bare, his face carefully unshaven, the more to impress them with.

And the boat grew – cupped between the hills, cushioned beneath a billowing sky – and we were seduced by the beauty of her lines, the rise and fall of her body, insinuating herself between hills and sky. And there were times when I lifted wood for Ben from a trailer that came up from the town, and sat in the yard and shared tea-breaks with them in the shadow of the boat. And Ben would seem oddly at peace, parked on his bum on the step, pipe between his teeth as he talked. But there were always echoes, moments when the truth would out, in the conjunction of a sentence, a hesitation in his eye, an insecurity with his words.

Cochise had begun to talk like him, and I saw him once, as he listened to her, shudder, and he blinked and rubbed his eyes as he realised that I had seen his fear and his hope in that unspoken moment. But what could I say?

The boat kept on growing. And I could see that he was torn between his fear that she might leave him and his fear that he would fail her, because he could not throw himself onto the open sea and could not trust her life in his hands. The power she had over him was the allure of her body and the strength of her personality. He could not believe that Cochise could want him for anything but the hope and promise that he had constructed for her, and he could not tell her of his failing, for fear that she would see him for what he was and leave him, although she knew his weakness well. If the boat sailed away, if they landed together on the opposite shore would that be the end or the beginning of their adventure? He wanted her to stay with him forever on top of this hill, hidden from the world. He was scared that Cochise was just another dream.

One day, that spring, we went walking over the hills overlooking the estuary in the late afternoon, the soft haze across the Irish sea, shimmers of light and cloud shadows across the bay, when we found Ben at the bottom of a gorge, fallen with his ankle twisted out of shape, broken. He called to us and I was surprised by his calm. We lifted and carried him between us, his arms around our shoulders, to the road, and Isabel sat with him on the verge, his leg on an outcrop of slate, while I walked to the phone and called for an ambulance. She rode with him to the hospital and I saw them disappear over the hill, merging into the light of evening in the valley, and I walked across the fields to the pub and the caravan to tell Cochise.

- Oh, no,

she said.

- How could he do that?

She sat on the steps of the caravan where Ben had drawn his map of the world in the dust the year before, and pulled her hair over her face so that I would not see what she was thinking.

- I wish he hadn't,

she said.

I saw him two or three days later, in the bar with a whisky

in his hand, and it seemed to me that a small cloud had lifted from the sky around him, that he was safe again.

- It was for the best,

he told us. And though the atmosphere had subtly changed, a calm fell over them as the year passed, and they settled back into the uncomfortable truce of winter, their cold caravan with the windows iced in the mornings, the steam of their kisses, the condensation from their cooking.

The calm lasted until just beyond the turning of the year, with the prospect of launching the boat nearing perceptibly through the months, and Ben's as yet unspoken insecurities re-emerging through the gloom of winter, like an octopus, tentacles grasping hair and clothes through the swirling sea, shadows of blue and green, ebbs and eddies that rocked the body in waves, tugging him down. His confidence fell through the floor of the sea, exploding in bubbles of nervous exhaustion that sprang to the surface, and left the water disturbed and ill at ease.

His nervousness was obvious to us, and to Cochise, who told us one night in the pub that she was worried about him. His worries chased him through his dreams, and he was jealous of anyone she spoke to, though she spoke to no-one he did not know. He worried about the boat and tried to keep it from her. He worried about the keel or the rudder, sitting up in bed with a start, afraid they would fail on the open sea. He worried about routes and the weather, and the storms to come. And when a sealed liferaft was delivered to him by someone from Bangor, he read the seals and the guarantees on the labels, and said to Cochise,

- What if it doesn't work?

As if ten thousand liferafts with the same make and name

had not already been delivered.
- Nobody would ever know,
he said.
- We could drown and nobody would know what had happened to us. How do you know it's not rotten inside?
- It has a certificate.
- That doesn't mean a thing.
- I'm sure it's alright,
she said, but when she woke the next morning he was already in the yard. She saw him walking across the gravel with the liferaft in his arms, and raced towards him and said,
- Don't, Ben.
    But he wouldn't listen.
- A liferaft is no use to us if we are dead,
he said, and dropped it in the field downwind of the pub. He pulled the cord and watched as the raft hissed and exploded, filling out and floating across the grass. The sheep ran from him, and the raft floated away across the fields. And when we asked Ben why he had done it, he said,
- Madoc didn't need a liferaft, did he?
before adding,
- Neither do I.
    He bought a rubber dinghy from a man in the town, and said he would keep it half-inflated on the deck of the boat, and if the boat ever looked like sinking he would jump into the dinghy and pump like a madman until the dinghy floated off.

    Come January or February, plans were in the air for putting the boat in the water in April of that year. Ben had found two crew who were willing to come for the ride. They would sail in June or July or August, progressing slowly across the Irish Sea and the Bay of Biscay for the Azores and Florida after the hurricane season was over.

Cochise was ecstatic. Her eyes and skin were bright with hope and anticipation for the moment she had worked for, and Ben seemed lighter and more at ease. The light of the coming spring shimmered on the underside of the clouds, the grass flowed along the hills, and the far-off birds span in ecstasy through the downfalling light.

The boat was almost there, the mast to be raised, the innards to be made comfortable within reason, some form of anti-fouling to be decided upon. Ben was proud of his handiwork. He said that he was ready to go, but there was still an inkling of doubt behind his eyes. He was not happy with his fate, but he could not say so. Suddenly his life was out of his hands and this was something he had not hoped for.

I saw him one evening in the pub and he had drunk himself into a stupor. He came back to the cottage after the pub had shut and sat with me, and told me he had had enough, and did I understand? I did. His eyes popped out of his head, his pipe in his mouth between the slur of his words.

- I wanted something else,

he told me, without defining what that might be, a gap between the thought and the expression of the thought that left everything unsaid.

- I dislike myself for what I have done,

he said, but I didn't listen, thinking that he was expressing a temporary doubt, brought on by drunkenness. We ended the night sitting on an outcrop of rock beneath the stars, Venus and the Big Dipper and a half moon, eaten out of shape by the shadow of the earth.

He fell asleep with a whisky bottle still in his hand just before the pale light of morning rose over the window ledge of the cottage, and I slept too in the armchair by the cold fire, waking at noon with a stiff neck and a sore shoulder. Ben was still asleep, and I made breakfast, and he stared at the fried egg like it was the devil staring back at him.

I didn't see him again. The next morning Cochise woke to find him gone, a note beside the bed, and nothing else. He wrote that it had all been a mistake, and wished her well. She was dignified, and said nothing to us. She stayed in the caravan for another month, but cancelled all their plans and went away.

And the boat and the caravan were left as monuments to his memory, the boat on stilts and the fragile and ancient caravan, until the storm came over the hills the following year and washed his dreams away.

'But love is gentle and love is kind
As to a jewel when first it's new
But love grows old and fades with time
And it fades away like morning dew'

The Spider and the Fly

The night porter had stubble on his chin and his jaw was oddly twisted. He had a glass eye. When he talked, it looked you over. I followed him with my bags in my hand as he took me through the half-lit corridors and stairs of the hotel. He stopped at the top of the stairs and took the fag from his mouth.
- You a student?
He bent his eye quizzically.
- No.
- Ah.

Satisfied, he screwed up his face, looked at the thin yellow fag in his hand, put it in his mouth, sucked it, and waited for me to pick up my bags. He walked sideways and pigeon-toed in a cloud of smoke.

My room was down the yard along a passage. We reached it down some greening steps by a drain that served half the hotel sinks and was plugged with tea leaves, slime and weeds. The room smelt damp, a smell of catpiss and fluff. The porter offered me a cup of tea but didn't come back with it. He was a solitary man, mean with words, lived in a room above the stables and slept all day.
- You'll be up at six tomorra,
he said.

The chef was different. When I think of him I think of those strange islands that erupt from the sea, olive-groves, lava, and the iguana. He was an elemental creature encrusted in stone. His shady blue skin hid crags and crevices, polyps and spitting boils.

- It is the God,

he would say, breathing deeply, straining every muscle in his frigid neck to release the tension, hanging like a hungry dog, strung on a tightening leash.

- It is good,

you would say of the food, and he would say,

- No, no, you only say it, but I know it,

and he would dig his nails into the lines of his face, and moan terribly, impossible to console, staring at the floor. His God was a dirty angel, obscured by clouds, casting wide nets into the sea, who tricked him with pathos and wit and tangled him in guilt.

- You live for nothing. It is to die,

he would say.

- The God, he knows. He is leading you all,

and you would feel guilty because you could not feel like him. How could he care so much, about God, about food, about where the olive oil had been left the night before?

- It's only a job,

you wanted to say,

- You've only got one life.

But, for the chef, every motion, every meal, was another step along the road to perfection, and perfection was an obsession beyond the self. He didn't care how we felt, that his walks through the everyday storm turned our lives into a daily hell; that we staggered towards the end of every day, hating him and his food and his God. It would not have mattered so much if the day ever dawned when the kitchen had been cleaned to his liking or the sauce tasted as it was meant to taste. You wanted somebody to grab him by the throat and shake him and say,

- Shut up,

but he wouldn't have understood anyway. We were the blemish that crossed the sun each morning and dimmed his horizon. What matter if someone told him to shut up? He was still the boss.

- I am the boss,

he would say,

- because I understand. You are nothing.

And it was true. I was nothing. I was a dishwasher, and my job was to be there at six in the morning, to keep the plates spinning through the soap in the sink, piled up to dry in the racks, and throw the pans under the taps and keep them moving back across the kitchens towards the chef.

He was malicious and without compassion. He would erupt coldly, wreaking his vengeance on the scullions who mopped the floors, stirred the soups, cut the vegetables and scraped the pans. A Spanish lad who came to learn English worked in the kitchens for two days and went to the toilet, unknowingly out of turn, and was sacked. He couldn't believe it. He had no money and nowhere to go. The chef pointed at the door and he left in tears. Later he came back and knelt on the floor, pleading and crying, tugging at the chef's sleeve, but the chef turned his back on him and looked the other way.

- He should have looked out,

he said,

- The God is cruel. He doesn't care. You see the spider. He gobbles the fly. No care. For me it is the same.

She was a student who worked upstairs, cleaning the

rooms and changing the beds. I met her on my way to steal a towel from a guest room. I told her what I was doing and she laughed. Her hair tied in a knot, she sat still at the window, looking out on the damp yard under the kitchens. She wanted to talk, talked. Best not to count on it, scrutinise the form. The day lapped at the glass, receded, and we conversed with the dark, diffuse precision clarifying shadow. The words were clear, rich and slow.

We walked out on the beach in the falling daylight when there was no-one about. The pebbles crunched by the sea at our feet. Winged creatures stirred and flapped at the shadows. I felt the tide coming in, hot on my tongue, and her lips were soft and warm. We sat on a bench looking out to sea, with our arms around our shoulders, and I felt a melancholy shiver and an uncertainty that the wind blew in.

- Do you fancy me?

she said.

- I don't know,

I said.

- What do you mean?

- I don't know.

- I don't have to.

- No.

We slept together in my room facing the yard. It was a cold damp place. Everything was flat blue or grey, washes of colour, silence. The nylon sheets stuck to our bodies and the noise from the yard kept us awake, but I liked her.

The days were slow. I rose with the sun colouring the sky. Jeans and socks screwed up on the floor. A reminding knock on the door. The aching light scratched the window. I would lean against the sink and rub the clouds of the previous night from my eyes. Days were like this, a strange affair, blurred and motionless. Dustbins tipped over, wrappers strewn. Bird's Eye. Wall's, walls, Bachelor's, fishbones, tea-leaves.

Outside the window the yard was slab coloured, clouded at the rim of the glass like a Daguerreotype negative.

- Where were you last night?

- With her.

- The chef's angry.

- Why?

- You're late.

- Only five minutes.

The chef shouted at one of the kitchen porters, and I walked past, trying to blend into the background and be unnoticed.

- You are useless,

he told the porter.

- And you,

he turned on me.

- You are the worst.

Pots and plates and pans. All I thought about all day long was pots and plates and pans. It had a curious effect on me. I stood over the sink in a self induced trance, moving the plates from side to sink to draining board in a vague and rhythmic dance, thankful at least that I wasn't one of the scullions who danced to the chef's tune and scrubbed the floors on their knees.

- You are a useless pig. You no enjoy work?

- No.

- Stupid. I want shine.

Waking up was more difficult with each new day,

especially when she was lying next to me, soft and warm, and she didn't have to get up for another hour. I would lie there and sniff her breath, her soft flesh next to mine, the smell of her hair, unwilling to move.

One morning there was a loud knock on the door. It woke me with a start. I was asleep, slept in again.

- Wake up.

- I'm coming.

- The chef's mad with you.

I rolled over her and pulled on my jeans and shirt and crawled out of the room, still trying to flatten my hair with my hand and to push the tails of my shirt into the top of my jeans. I ran into the yard, up the back steps and into the kitchen, eyes half-open, lids slipping shut, and affected an air of nonchalant indifference I did not have, but he saw me.

- Out,

he shouted, standing back on his heels, swaying. I smiled at him.

- You're having me on.

His face flickered, the temperature rising.

- Out.

- No way,

I said, trying not to catch his eye, and walked round him to the sink. I ran the tap, and tested the water with my fingers.

- This is no good,

he said, untying his apron and throwing it onto the bench. He sat on one of the kitchen chairs.

- You go, or I cook no more,

he said, and waited as I began to wash the plates,

- I cook no more,

he said, and folded his arms. He gave me half a day to pack

84

my things and leave.

She hid me in her room, but it was difficult. The housekeeper slept in the room next but one to her, and we had to talk in whispers and never be seen as we came and went, which was hard, because the housekeeper was always tramping around the corridors in a flurry of bedsheets and pillows. During the days, when she was working, making the beds in the upstairs rooms, I had to go out.

I spent the last of my money trying to find a job in the area, knocking on doors and hanging round the back entrances of hotels. I went to the employment, sat beneath the warning posters and waited to be called. The clerk was a small man with a flop of hair that had been swept across his balding pate. He faced me with an air of resignation and futility.

- I want to sign on.
- You haven't filled in your address.
- I haven't got one.
- Why?
- I just don't.
- You have to have an address to sign on.
- Not without money I won't get one.
- Where you staying?
- I cannot say.
- Well, I can't help you.
- How'm I supposed to eat? I want a job.
- Well?
- You give the winos money. Why not me?
  I stood up and pushed back my chair.
- I'll not be an apprentice,
I said.

She had no more money than I did. She brought back whatever food she was able to find, but she had no reason to be in the kitchens and pilfering the leftovers was not easy. One evening she came back with nothing and we lay still on her bed, curtains open as the dark fell around us. We watched the clouds and it began to rain, slowly across the roof of the wing of the hotel, penetrating everything, over-spilling a blocked drainpipe and gushing out of the corner, splattering loudly in the yard below.

When the rain stopped I said,

- I know what I will do.

I went along the corridor beside the housekeeper's room, down the stairs and along the passage to the yard to raid the kitchen store. The yard was streaked with shadow. I hid behind the steps and watched as one of the scullions went down into the cellar and came out with something in his hand. He locked the door behind him, and switched the yard light off as he went back into the kitchens. I could hear the distant bang and clatter of falling pans, and the chef's angry shout.

- No. No.

- Where is the ladle?

- Here, give it to me. I will show you.

I ran across the yard and pushed the door but it would not move. The kitchen door came open. It was another one of the scullions, stood in the light while the chef shouted at him. He crossed the yard to the store, and I moved back into the shadows. He fumbled with the keys, swearing, and I thought for a moment that he might see me.

- Fuckin' cook,

I heard him say, and he banged about inside the store,

shifting boxes here and there. He came out with his hands full, and pulled the door shut with his foot. He tried to lock it, but couldn't reach the key.

- Bastard,

he said, and I waited as he stumbled across the yard into the kitchens, the boxes in his hands overbalancing him as he shoved the door open with his foot.

I pushed the door into the store and it came open. I felt my way around the shelves in the dark, anxious in case he returned, and grabbed what tins I could. A tin fell, clattered onto the floor. Footsteps. A sound in the yard, closer than the kitchen din. I pushed myself back into the shadows. Somebody moved in the doorway.

- Who's there?

a voice said, but I didn't speak. Stood stark still. It was the night porter and he was scared.

- I know you're there,

he said. The light from his torch flickered nervously up and down the shelves and landed on my shoe. His voice trembled.

- Who is it?
- Shush,

I said,

- It's only me.
- Who? What? Student. Get out.
- Just a couple of cans.
- No. Get out. Me job.

He grabbed my shoulder and pushed me.

- Wait on.
- No.
- One tin?
- Get lost,

he said, and I scrambled across the yard, still clutching what tins I had. There was a tin of prunes and a tin of peaches and a tin of baked beans.

Back in her room later that night, she lay naked across the chair, scratching her leg and smoking. I lay on her bed on my side, my head in my hand, wondering at her lack of self-consciousness, her stomach pouting slightly through the shadows. I said to her,
- Why don't you come with me?
- I can't,
she said.
- You can.
- No.
- Why not?
- You've got no money.
- That doesn't matter.
- It does.
- I'll get a job.
- I can't.

We left at first light next morning. She didn't leave a note or tell anyone she was leaving. We snuck out through the corridors with our bags over our shoulders, and stood at the roadside in the first grey light of day.

A lorry stopped. The driver was glum, elbow steep on the wheel, read the *Sun* on the boards. The sun on the roof, burnt. We sat high in the cab, and watched the road as it came towards us, a long black snake of oil and tar.

Goods Train

At evening when the light begins to fade, I am on the steps of
the guard's van of a train that is racing into the night. My feet
are balanced precariously on the steps. My hand grabs the
rail and the wind tears at my hair and my clothes. I am adrift
in a moving world. The wind blows the sounds of the diesel
down the tracks towards me. The trucks rattle and dance
between the rails. A spark catches me in the eye and I duck
inside the van and wipe it away with the back of my hand.

On the lines that I travel my direction has been laid for me.
The rails bend into the river and the river yards, and I follow
them, a bird, smothered by my own steam, banging my
wings against the buffers. I follow the tracks of the wind and
leave a trail of broken feathers scattered along the lines.

My wings are axles. My heart is a boiler, and I believe I am
free.

In the morning the light floats in at half past six, touching
the clouds and the glass, first words frosted in air. Still asleep,
her mouth snatching air, her arm breaking sideways,
clutching at air. I touch her lips and she moans. I touch her
hips and she begins to stir. I throw the blankets over her, and
stand naked by the electric fire and shiver. I wash in the cold
light-streaked water and pull my trousers and shirt on.

There is a frost on the hard earth. The pavement is iced and
the trees shiver. I walk beneath the shadows of the railway
viaduct and the church. The cold sun brings with it strange
effects on the fringes of the clouds, melts the crispness of the
air with a slow and biting warmth, stirs life into these cold

89

and empty streets, soothes my aching bones. And the trains zoom into three-quarter picture, too quick for the eye to catch. They pound the rails and carry the morning forward.

I climb Lovers' Walk Sidings and cross the lines and points to the signalbox. A train is standing there, ready for the off. Thirty empty trucks and a thrumming diesel locomotive. The guard is walking between the tracks, checking the couplings and the brakes, stamping his feet and blowing into his hands. I am early and stop for a smoke. He says how cold it is. He had a derailment last week. A wagon came off the rails and blocked the up fast. They kept him up half the night and most of the morning after. They had him by the knackas. I nod and laugh. I stub my cigarette out between the sleepers and wave to him as he goes.

I walk to the station with my hands in my pockets. I hunch my jacket around my shoulders. I kick a stone through the railings. I have my pass that gets me through the ticket barriers with a picture of myself, a studied smile and unseeing eyes and a bait-box to keep my sandwiches in. I am the man with the flag on the train, and when I am out on the tracks I have no-one to listen to but myself. I follow the machinery of the stars with a flag and a coloured lamp. I am Dostoevsky with a sandwich box. I am Magellan with a signal lamp. And in my tea breaks I count the tiles and dream of her. I wonder if she is waking now, rubbing her body down, and cycling to work in that trance of blue air.

The music is deafening, crashing steel on granite. On the forecourt people jaywalk in front of taxis and weave through porters with trolleys. The sound is terrible. The sky has been torn open with wretched hands and bleeds. Smoke and glassy sunlight cut through stone. I go to the locker room and change my clothes. I wear the uniform jacket and a pair of jeans. I never wear the tie.

Boots is leaning against the wall and sweeps the floor. His uniform is stained and has marks on it, but his shoes always shine. He walks deliberately so as not to scuff them. He walks with his head bowed so as to watch them.

His body barely seems to move as he sweeps the floor. He strikes an elaborately lethargic pose and holds it, from elusive movement to deceptive stance. His brush barely touches the floor. It gives the dust a reasonable chance.

He has one eye on his shoes and one eye on the clock. In the morning he checks the rota with a twisted finger and says,
- I'll not do that,
- Nor tha',
- Nor tha',
- Nor tha',
and walks away.

The cafe in Gloucester Road opens at seven in the morning. The blinds go up and let the smoke in. The kettle goes on the boil, and Boots sits at a table in the corner with *The Sporting Life*.

The atmosphere thickens and the workers come and go. They will eat their food and drink their tea and he will still be there, balancing his bets, crossing off the winners and the losers, watching the smoke rise from his cigarette, killing time.

The clock in the station is brass and hangs from the girders. At the end of the shift the men stand in a line by the door and watch the slow, black hand move through the minutes, and Boots will be the first in line with his bag and his paper in his hand, ready for the off.

91

Richard Hillesley

The train leaves at half past seven and the sun spills across the lines. I sway between the tracks and the dust-flecked wind rips through my hair and clothes, beneath me ballast and the silver rails. The morning comes over the land and the trees are a blur, and the wagons in sidings and the passing trains and the shed by the tracks where I began my training as a guard. I spent a week sitting at a tidy desk in a row of desks with the trains flashing past. The teacher was a retired engine driver who asked us why we had come, and we said,
- I was out of work,
or
- I like trains,
or
- The employment sent me and I needed the money, except Riley, at the end of the row, who said,
- I couldn't think of anything better to do.
- If you work hard, Riley, you could become an engine driver, said the engine driver, and Riley slid further down into his chair, resolute and slack.
- I don't want to be an engine driver,
he said.
- Why not?
- My dad's an engine driver and I know what it's like.
- But what will you do with your life, lad?
- Go to work, go home, get drunk and sleep it off,
he said.

For all that I saw him a few months later hanging off the back of a goods train with a flag and a lamp on the up line as I passed him on the down. Riley had become a second man, and was training to be an engine driver. When I spoke to him during a shunt in a yard a few days later, he said he liked it.

He rides in the cab, and sometimes he gets to drive the train, racing into the night with the rails coming up to meet him. He is a friend in a way, and sometimes we meet for a drink or a coffee after a shift, or he comes round with his girlfriend of an evening for a spliff. I like him well enough and I don't mind him coming round, but he only has to sit in a room and it looks untidy, and he always takes an age to leave. He licks another Rizla and rolls another spliff and leaves behind a trail of ash and smoke that hangs around for days.

The wind has shifted. It is crisp and carries the smells of evening, smoke and dried leaves. In the trees it blows hot and cold. It crackles on the panes, and I lie on our bed and touch my toes with one hand, and cup my head in the other. The fire is warm. The heat rises towards the ceiling. We should lie in hammocks between the lightbulbs. We should float among the stars.

I intoxicate myself with the smell of the rain as it drums upon the path. She sits on the bed and draws the kittens that were born in the bag under the television on Christmas Day. She picks up a roach from the bed and flicks it on the fire. It has burnt a small but perfect hole in the bed covers, and she gives me an accusing look.

- What?

I say.

- Don't deny it,

she says, but I know it was Riley.

- Why pick on him?

she says.

- Because he did it,

I say.

Richard Hillesley

- But I like him,
she says, and I move across the bed and watch a streak of rain
rolling down the glass.

On the last evening of the night shift I am on the steps of
the guard's van. The driver's name is Joe. The second man is
Riley. Joe slows down by Lovers' Walk Sidings and Riley
jumps down from the cab, steps between the tracks and gives
an elaborate wave to me as he walks across the sleepers to the
stairs. He is on his way home. He has clocked on, but Joe has
let him go for the night. Joe will clock him off at the end of his
shift. A second man is a tiring distraction, and there's a long
night ahead. Riley goes home and Joe has the cab to himself,
and he can dream.

A train of empties. A diesel locomotive and…. Fivesix-
seven ……. Fourteenfifteensixteen. Eighteennineteentwenty
wagons and a guard's van. We're taking the train to a goods
yard forty miles up the line, where the wagons will be
shuffled in tidy rows, like a pack of cards.

The rails curve behind the stone piles, the cranes and the
elevators, and I hang from the van. A light flashes between
the wheels. The screech of a hot axlebox, and the engine
sways between the lines. I stand on the platform at the back
of the van and stare into the dark. When the engine slows I
turn the wheel and apply the brakes. The van slithers and
screeches, stretching the couplings out. The stove glows in
the night. The leaves spell out their tales and the trucks move
between shadows. I warm my hands and think of her.

The wheels of the train rock and jangle like a jazz piano.
The wagons swing to the rhythm of the rails and the engine
blows like a saxophone sliding down the stars, taking my

breath away. Everywhere there is chaos, and through the chaos there is harmony, the bang of buffers in sidings, the crash of points, the hum of tunnels, the sound of falling pots and pans cascading from a metal bridge as we pass below, and the pinheads of light and flood of colours as the train comes out the other side.

I am almost asleep. The bang and rattle of the van shakes me awake. I roll myself a cigarette. The taste is on my lips. The smoke blows around my face. I cannot sleep during the day. At the end of a week on night shift I am walking on borrowed legs and the tiredness chills me. I take a second jersey from my bag and pull it over my head. A blue flash from an electric train on the opposite line, lightbulbs, hats, and faces in the moving windows. Snow drifts down through the trees. I pour a cup of shaken coffee from my flask. The smell is intoxicating, but the fact isn't equal to the promise. It has a dull and cloudy flavour that lines my mouth and inhibits my sense of taste.

I am not expecting the crash when it comes. The shriek of steel against steel, the snap of breaking iron and a sound like a factory chimney falling into the rubble. The van shudders and I am thrown sideways. The breath is sucked out of me. My ribs feel like they are cracked and it hurts to breathe. I come round slowly and I am on the floor.

I crawl to the back of the van and slowly find my feet. The track is empty behind us. I shine my torch along the train. Three of the wagons are off the rails. An axle is spinning, suspended over a sleeper in the snow. Two of the wagons have scissored across the up fast. The train is derailed.

Joe is out of the cab and standing by the signal. The rails are singing. A train on the down fast is racing towards us. I jump down from the van and limp along the track towards the engine. The rumble of the oncoming train is getting louder. I wave my lamp as it flashes past, smudges of light in the windows, heavy wheels and a flash of steel, a galloping horse between the tracks, the train blows his horn and fades away, swishing along the rails, breathing ice and fire through the cold night air, leaving a hole in the silence behind.

By the time I reach the engine Joe is ringing the signalbox.
- Stop the trains,
he shouts.
- Put the signals on red.

We're in trouble. Riley's thirty miles away, and we need him here.

I run up and down the line putting caps on the rails. They explode under the wheels of oncoming trains and alert the drivers to the danger on the line. Joe runs to the signalbox, and gets the signalman to ring the breakdown unit and a number for Riley, but Riley can't be found. He isn't at home. Joe has Riley's girlfriend on the phone, but she doesn't know where he is. She thinks he's in the pub, and we're in trouble. He's supposed to be with us, and if he doesn't get here we are out of a job.

We don't care about the still and silent train stuck on the line a few hundred yards further back. Nothing can be done about that until the crane and the spotlights arrive. It is cold outside and I am shivering. Ice on the tracks. Snow on the branches. The night is luminous. The train shines white and black along the line and shivers in the moonlight. In the distance the lights of a town sit in the curve of the hills, and the reflection of the town glows on the underside of the clouds.

The phones in the signalbox don't stop ringing. Everyone up and down the line wants to speak to us, but none of them are Riley. Riley's girlfriend rings us back. She has found him and he's in a taxi and on his way to join us, but he has 30 miles to go, racing through the snow in a taxi in the dark. We can't make him move faster, and the breakdown train and the crane are on their way.

The signalman knows the score and rings the next box up the line to ask him to slow the train. Everyone between here and the end of the line knows our plight, and everyone is doing their best to make sure we're OK, but it makes no difference because Riley still isn't here. Riley's taxi and the breakdown train are in a race through the night, and the air is anxious and cold because there's nothing we can do to make him get here quicker. So we make a cup of tea, and I go outside for a piss in the snow.

The sky is ice-blue, blue-black, and spectral. The clouds are collapsing and the night is falling around me, and I am shaking it off and pulling up my flies when I look up the line and see the breakdown train coming down the track towards me, huge in the night and getting bigger as it closes in on me, horn blowing through the snow.

Riley is still not here. I run up the stairs to warn Joe, but he already knows. Within minutes an inspector and a guard are in the box, asking us why our train has come off the line. Joe is telling them and I'm looking out the window through the snow for Riley when I see a taxi slither into the yard below. Riley jumps out of the passenger seat, pulling his coat on sideways, gets in a tangle. I wonder if he's drunk, but he runs for the door and comes up the stairs of the signalbox, looking sensible, and drifts across the room. He sees that Joe is busy, tries to be unnoticed and slides along the window and stands against the radiator beside me, slipping a mint under his tongue. They haven't said anything to him and we think we may have got away with it.

But, just as we begin to relax, the taxi driver appears at the top of the stairs.

- Hey,

he says, and I grab him and push him back through the door.

- Shush,

I say,

- I'll give you your money.

But he wants to haggle. And I have to follow him out the door and down the steps to the taxi. Standing in the snow, looking up at the window, hoping the inspectors won't see me or the taxi driver and guess why he's here.

- Not fun you know,

he says.

- driving all this way.

And I agree. I give him the money for the fare, and a little bit extra.

- Is that all?

he says.

- I haven't got any more,

I say. Riley's still standing in the window, looking down at me. I've put my job on the line for him, and now I'm paying his taxi fare.

- Tight bastard,

says the taxi driver to me as he pulls away.

- Aye. Right,

I say into the snow. I have given him the last of my change.

Six or seven hours later the inspectors let me go. It is almost light and I am a passenger on the first train of the day, travelling backwards along the line, watching the tracks and the trees disappear behind me. I'm still annoyed at Riley and he still owes me for the taxi fare. The light floats in through the window, expanding imperceptibly, teasing its way around the corners, nudging the shadows back into the cracks, sending shivers down my spine, giving restless form to a restless world that is always moving away from me, changing shape and renewing itself.

As I turn out of the station and into Gloucester Road I see Boots. He is walking towards the cafe and staring at his shoes. He looks at me knowingly, and says,
- Riley's a lucky lad.

I don't know how he knows. How can he know? He touches his nose, and suggests he knows everything. I walk home through the slush on the ground, beneath the shadows of the railway viaduct and the church, the first light of the sun warming the edges of the streets. I put my key in the lock and go to bed just before she rises.

When the morning comes, I lie with my head on the pillow and watch her as she flicks her hand through her hair with long and sinuous fingers, washing behind the ears, staring into the mirror, standing on one leg to pull her knickers on. This must be love.

My wings touch the corners and the world falls away and I hold my hands and count my fingers. Who knows what might be waiting for me down a few sidings more? She moves around the room, steps into her skirt and pulls her blouse over her head. She's ready to go to work and brushes

me on the cheek.
- Riley was here last night,
she says, as she tugs at the seam of her skirt.
- ?
- He tried it on with me,
she says, and walks towards the door. And I am suddenly
awake.

A Gap of Cloud

Gwynfor stood with his back to the sky, a field away from where we were. The wind rose from the valley and bit into his side. His eyes were a dark line under his brow. The gun in his hands glinted in the sunlight. Behind him the house and a stream that fell straight from the clouds.

We saw him when we came over the hill, legs apart, hair and clothes blown sideways by the wind. He lifted the gun to his shoulder and fired. The sound followed after the smoke, and Isabel fell in the grass, her hand and her skirt rising through the sky as she fell, and I ran towards her, thinking she had been hit.

- Why did he do that?

she said.

- To scare us,

I said. He moved in gestures through the wind as he came towards us, his massive face beneath his cap, dark eyes beneath the crevice of his brow. He stopped by the wall to pick something up.

- Rabbit,

he said, and his lips stretched across his mouth in the shape of a smile.

The past repeats itself through the seasons, in the wind and the rain and the rush and chuckle of the streams. Clouds hanging over the mountains, fields obscured by mist, a landscape that is harsh and soft, cold and indifferent. At Bryn Hyfrid, on a corner by his land past the ruins of the quarrymen's cottages, there are the remains of a bronze age hut circle in a field, set at angles. Further to the east there is a line of stones and one at the end of the row, standing on its own and taller than the rest.

Not that it mattered, because nobody knew or cared except the walkers and Gwynfor himself, but when we told him we were going to see the circle and the stones, he said,
- A stone is just a stone,
as if that was all there was to say.

And when we were up there among the stones we could see him across the valley, herding his sheep from inside his Land Rover, perched on the diagonal tracks between the gateposts and the irregular walls, watching us and whistling to his dogs on the opposite slope. The sheep swarmed in circles. The shadows of clouds left pools of light across the fields. And Gwynfor leant against the door of his Land Rover, his body like a landslip on the Berwyns, looking up at us.

I waved to him but he made no response. And when we left the stones he started up the Land Rover. We could hear the noise and bang of the gears as he pushed the vehicle down the tracks. He sat at the wheel, his arm out the window, slapping the door as he passed us, and accelerated loudly as he pulled away, shouting at us inaudibly. And when we passed him a few minutes later, he was back there with his gun and his dogs.

When we told them in the village, they laughed and said,
- Well, what did you expect?

Gwynfor was part of the landscape, a chip off the mountain, at home in the fields. He moved like the seasons, slowly and deliberately, merging into the landscape, a simple farmer, circumscribed by the hills, the drystone walls and the clouds. And we were incomers. What did we expect? He didn't like us and he didn't like the stones. The stones had a mystery and a purpose of their own and belonged in a way that he never could. He wanted us to leave him alone and the stones to go away.

That evening we saw him in the pub, standing at the bar in his boots and his work clothes. He had the rabbit in a bag in his hand and slapped it on the bar.
- Something for the pot,
he said to the landlord, and turned to look at us.
- Rabbit,
he said, throwing a note of dissonance into the air. He was pleased with himself, and wanted us to know it. He had few words but he coughed and scraped and threw us glances just to let us know he was there. And when he left the bar to go to the toilet he came past us and whispered in Isabel's ear,
- Shut up, you,
though she had said nothing. She pushed him away, and though she hadn't meant it, he fell to the floor among the coats and chairs, unbalanced by her indignation. I tried to help him to his feet but he wouldn't let me.

He put one hand on the floor and one on a chair and lifted himself up and shook his head as he walked away to the toilets in the yard, leaving us to deal with the silence and the stares around the room. The only one hurt was me, kicked on the shin by her when I tried to come between them. A few minutes later, he came back into the room with another rabbit in his bag and threw it on the table in front of us.
- Rabbit,
he said, and bared his teeth, barely a grin, and left a threat hanging in the air.
- You'll see,

103

he said, and walked away.

One evening, not long after, when the sun was sinking through a low wet mist, stirrings of a storm in the clouds, John Evans saw Gwynfor on the side of the hill, his Land Rover perched at an angle through the wind, stretching a rope between the Land Rover and one of the stones. John said to him,
- I wouldn't do that,
and Gwynfor said,
- You don't believe that stuff,
though he wasn't sure himself. There were stories about the stones that had been passed down through the generations and left a doubt lingering in the air.
- But I do,
said John.
- I don't believe you,
said Gwynfor, and tied the rope around the stone and twisted the other end around the tow-bar. The stone seemed to give a fraction, but the rope was old and weak and snapped as he pulled the vehicle forward.

John, leaning on his stick, said nothing. And Gwynfor threw the Land Rover down the hill, shouting at John above the noise of the engine as he went, harsh words lost in the storm of evening.

After that we went out of our way to watch the stones just to be sure. One day we saw Gwynfor high in the trees over the top field, watching us, a wisp of smoke rising behind him from a fire he had made, his gun in his arms. He lifted it to his shoulder and pointed it in our direction, making as if to shoot. But he didn't. And the stones stood still and silent, streaked with moss and lichen, aching through the mist.

At times like this it was easy to believe the myths, to feel something in the wind, but we knew that the stones were only stones and the mists were only mists. A line of stones on the side of a hill like pieces in a children's game, a stone dropped here, a stone dropped there, and the ancient field boundaries mapped out like the squares on a children's gaming board, F sharp minors and stunted fifths, walking at angles and leaning on the wind. I would pull my scarf more tightly round my face and stamp my feet hard on the ground just to feel the earth beneath.

Gwynfor moved the stones early one morning when no-one was about, when the stars were out and the sun was just a shadow of itself, when his breath made shapes in the air and the grass flopped with dew. Two of the stones were pulled from the ground and discarded there. Another he towed across the fields with his tractor and left among the gorseclumps just above his house, to pave his yard.

That night we met at John's to do something about it though we didn't know what we could do. The rain had begun to fall, splattering through the leaves and drains, rushing over the pebbles and moss, lifting the river over its banks. We walked over the hill towards the stones, six or seven of us, torches in our hands, stumbling on the rough ground, to put the stones back where they belonged. Two of the stones lay on their side, where Gwynfor had left them. We pushed and pulled by the light of our torches and we were lucky and they fell back into place.

The rain had stopped and the moon shone through a gap

in the clouds as we went down the hill to Gwynfor's place to move the other stone. But it wouldn't move. The stone was too big and we were too few. And Gwynfor, disturbed by our noise, came out and watched us as we walked away, the last stone still lying there among the clumps of gorse. He had won, or so we thought until two weeks later when Gwynfor came visiting.

I saw him first from our upstairs window, pale in the gloom of the smoke from the bonfire that Isabel had lit in the garden. His jacket hung from his body limp as washing in the wind, and a confusion of submission and defiance made war with his body and his clothes. He wouldn't come in but something was on his mind. Isabel moved towards him and I followed her. He cocked his head to one side, cap in hand, scratched his scalp, and said,
- You did it, didn't you?
The stone had been taken the previous night and was nowhere to be seen.
- It was you that did it, wasn't it?
he said, his voice suddenly thin and cold, like the wind in the winter trees. We hadn't seen the stone since last we saw him and our car couldn't have made it up to his farm. But he didn't believe us, because if it wasn't us it must have been magic.
- It must have been you,
he said, and left us, his face plumbed of feeling. He walked up the lane and became a shadow on the distant hill.

We went to Bryn Hyfrid one morning not long after, when spring was flushing out the trees and the heavy streams and the soft sunlight touched the grass on the mountains with warmth, and the stones were all in place, even the one that we had left in the gorse. It had found its way back to its place in the row.

Gwynfor watched us from the line of trees by the top field, his shotgun cradled in his arms. He walked towards us, his dogs running behind him, and we stood by the stones, and watched him as he came.

- It was you that did it, wasn't it?

he said, and we told him it wasn't. We really didn't know how it had happened. So he knew it was magic and the feeling left him pale and empty, as if his life had spilled into the stones. His instinct was to lift his gun to his shoulder, and to twist his body around to take aim at the trees and us and the stones. And I yelled,

- No,

at the top of my voice, thinking that he would do something crazy, but he turned slowly, lifted the gun towards the clouds, and fired at the empty sky above us.

Richard Hillesley

Marlon on The Streets

After school we ran through the streets under a pale sky, snotnosed and tufthaired, pushing and squawking like the gulls over the fish quay at evening.

- Dare yis.
- Bet yis.
- Na, yi won't.

But we did. Diving into the swirling waters with our wings splayed and our mouths wide open, webbed feet alighting on the rails, screaming into the cold air, and swooping behind doorways to pick up scraps. We broke the windows of our own homes and rebelled against our own kind.

- Bet yis.
- Na.
- Gan on.

And if we didn't know what we were doing it didn't stop us, running with the others through the streets with our quivers filled with arrows, our arrows barbed with hard words, and our cheeks inflated with barefaced cheek.

- Bet yis.
- Na.
- Gan on.

The things we saw were hidden from schoolbooks and copied essays, the wrecks and bones washed up on the tide and the faces in the coming storm. But it never seemed so bad then. Our lives were a textbook in acquiescence and submission. We broke the windows of our own homes and rebelled against our own kind, running in the dusk down by the river, sliding down the side of the wind, fighting over scraps until the night fell across the houses and the storms stirred the waves.

- Bet yis.

- Na.

- Gan on,

screaming into the cold air.

One evening we were playing football in the back lane after school when Vinnie came down the lane, hopping between the bins, cocky and knowing with a skip in his step like Albert Finney in *Saturday Night and Sunday Morning*, and walked straight through our game. He tackled Jimmy and pushed away the skinny kid with glasses who lived in the flats at the end of the street. He shimmied past a couple of us with the ball at his feet and kicked it over the wall into the builder's yard, where he knew we wouldn't be able to get it back. He was ten or fifteen years older than us, and we couldn't stop him doing it.

- You didn't have to do that,

Jimmy said. But he did it anyway.

- I did it, didn't I?

he said and kept on walking.

- Bully,

someone shouted, but he didn't care. He had no self-awareness and couldn't help himself. He lived down the street from us, worked at the second hand car lot on the piece of wasteland at the end of Church Row, bombed out during the Second World War. The wasteland belonged to his brother and his gang, filled with clapped out 'good runners', Zephyrs and Victors and Anglias and Consuls with their prices whitewashed onto the windscreens.

Vinnie's brother was older than he was, and worked as a fixer for the gang. They ran the fair and traded in slot machines and one armed bandits. They wanted to be gangsters but were bikers and small town bullies playing at being something greater than they were. Vinnie spent his days in the shed on the car lot and waited for punters, coming out of the door every now and then to make shapes and shadow box with the clouds and stars, or to bully kids like us.

One ordinary evening, under a black and white sky, we ran past the lot and one of us had the idea that it would be a laugh to climb over the car bonnets and fix the prices written on the windscreens by rubbing out the last nought, to teach him a lesson.
- Bet yis.
- Na.
- Gan on,
Jonah said, and I went. And Mel and Jonah laughed as I climbed under the advertising hoardings and the fence and ran through the gravel and the oil stained puddles, circled in silver and black. I could see the yellow light in the hut and Vinnie inside yawning and stretching as the shadows lengthened across the lot.

I had done this before, but even so I was tingling and scared like you are when you do something wrong and you know you might be caught. The game was to run between the cars without Vinnie seeing us. I crept up to a Zephyr next to the hut, and sprawled over the bonnet, watching him through the glass of the windscreen, scratching my arm on a wiper that caught my sleeve as I rubbed out the nought at the end of the price. I jumped out of sight and fell onto my knees.

110

- Bastards,

I whispered, and crawled to the next car and turned to see
Mel and Jonah laughing and pointing. Vinnie was coming out
of the hut, standing in the cold in his T-shirt, sweat-stained
and oilstreaked, his chest puffed out, his hands stiff in his
pockets. I looked up and saw Dolores coming down the street
in her clicketyclack shoes, tight sweater and high-pointed bra.
Dolores was his girlfriend, and he came out towards the car I
was leaning on and yelled,

- Hoo, pet,

and she waved and said,

- Ooh, Marlon.

And I slipped down and crawled to the end of the row,
skipping round the back of the next car on all-fours so she
wouldn't be able to see me, and slipped away between the
cars and over the fence and under the advertising hoarding.
Jonah said,

- She called him Marlon.

- Marlon?

- Aye.

Vinnie's jaw was long and twisted and his eyes were like
onion rings dipped in gravy. He wore a white T-shirt and
jeans turned up at the bottom just like Terry Malloy in *On the
Waterfront*. But he was no Marlon Brando.

In those days the lads liked to stand on street corners,
looking hard and flicking their hair. They wore drapes and
drainpipes and switched back Van Goghs, waxed in axle-
grease and layered in careful wads. The combs in back-
pockets were as necessary as a wound to a thrill, and Vinnie
was a boxer, though he'd never made it past the gym and a
few local fights. He cut imaginary silhouettes across the

evening sky and boxed with the shadows as he came down the street, curling his lip and flicking his hand through his hair, making a stand against the weather and tearing the sky apart.

His bike was a BSA Shooting Star. It was beaten up, needed a lot of work and cost him very little, but it was his pride and joy. He carried a flick knife and curled his lip. He was always in trouble and having fights, and he told my friend Billy once he got more of a thrill from a fight than from getting laid.

- He didn't.
- Aye, he did.

But he was no Marlon Brando. His land was the fairground, gum in his jaw, a world on his shoulders, *High Noon* by the Shore. Machines that whirred and whined through the night.

Ship matches. Packets of 5 Players' Weights.

Courting in the cinema pits. Dancing to 78s.

Six evenings a week, he took the bike apart, oil on the pavement and the parts laid out, and on the seventh he rode to the coffee bar or the fair and made angles along the handlebars to impress the girls. Dolores was his girlfriend. He treated her like dirt, but she hung on his every word. She was complicit in her own undoing, and said he was everything she wanted in a man. He was hard and could spit as far as heaven. He was everything she had ever dreamed of, but he was no Marlon Brando.

We stayed behind the advertising hoarding, looking to see if Vinnie had seen us, hoping he'd lose his rag and chase us up the street, but he didn't care about us, so we were happy to chase each other and kick a tin along the pavement until

Donnie came around the corner. Donnie was a friend of Vinnie's who lived in South Frederick Street. He joined us in our game, span around and scored a goal and walked away towards the car lot, saw the Zephyr, looked at the price and said he wanted it.

He knocked on the shed door and Vinnie came out and we kicked the can into touch, and watched through the fence to see if Vinnie had noticed we'd changed the price. He grabbed the keys from the shed and Donnie drove the car to the top of the street and back, feeling good.

- I'll take it,

he said, and handed over the cash. Vinnie looked the car over and said,

- The price doesn't look right,

but it was too late by then. The light slipped over the houses, hooked on the windows and the cranes of the shipyards, and we flew home, sliding down the side of the wind.

One evening a week or two later, as the grey light spilled over the houses and the lights came on, a Commer van drew up next to Vinnie's house, and two lads in leather jackets climbed out with club hammers and smashed up his bike. I almost felt sorry for him. He had given more love to his bike than he'd ever given to Dolores. No-one knew who they were or why they did it. Jonah thought it was to teach him a lesson for selling the Zephyr to Donnie. And some thought they were after Vinnie's brother.

A couple of days later, we saw his brother coming down the street and tried to tell him it wasn't Marlon but us who had fixed the price on the Zephyr. But it meant nothing to him.

113

Richard Hillesley

- Who's Marlon?

was all he said. And soon enough we knew there was other stuff going on. The times were exciting and filled with wonder, and something new was happening every day. One evening, we came upon the Commer van by the fish quay. It was a burnt out shell. The doors were blown open, and someone had ripped off the tyres. We swooped around it, looking for scraps, but there was nothing to tell us what had happened. All we knew was that the bikers were at war with each other, and Vinnie wasn't going to work on his own anymore. He always had two or three of his friends with him, sitting in the hut in leathers and jeans, looking hard and staring out of the window, their bikes lined up outside the window.

We were kids and to us it was the stuff of legend, but there were gaps between the myths we wanted to believe, of riders fading into the sunset carrying the world before them, and the reality of the streets, aimless stand-offs on stationary bikes, the bikers showing off and throwing insults at each other among the fading noise of screaming tyres and broken exhausts. Once or twice it went wrong and someone was hurt, but usually it was self-inflicted and they had no-one to blame but themselves.

The big news that summer was the big fight at the fair. A gang of bikers came out of the night, flailing chains and yelling, roaring and skidding between the rides, knocking people over and making a lot of noise, but they didn't do much harm. They scared some people, and a lot of stories were told in the days that followed. Some of the lads became heroes. One had hoyed a rock at one of the disappearing bikers and knocked the rider off his bike. Another had a piece of flying glass hit him in the face and it took out his eye. But it wasn't what people said it was. There was no big fight and nothing really changed.

After that things went quiet for a while. Once or twice some bikers came riding past the fair, shouting and whooping, but they faded back into the night as fast as they came, and Vinnie was on his own again. His biker mates had gone back to the fair to look out for the lads on the rides and Vinnie had to take care of himself. The troubles faded into memory and we thought it was over until the night of the fire.

It was a dark and murky night, mist and smoke coalescing over the houses as we played football in the street and a stream of bikers came skidding into the car lot in a storm of noise and burnt exhausts. We didn't know it at the time but they came with cans of petrol and lighted matches and threw them over the hut and the cars. When Vinnie came out of the hut they turned on him and beat him up. All we knew of it was the muffled explosions we could hear in the night, and the great plume of smoke rising from the yard as the cars caught fire. The bikes roared away and smoke and flames rose over the houses. No-one knew where Vinnie was until he emerged through the smoke, blackened and bloodstained, stumbling and falling up the lane, hanging onto Dolores' arm. The old men came out of the pub to see what was going on, and we stopped our game in the street and stood in a line as he went past. We didn't know what else to do or say, and Jimmy said,

- Wey hey, Marlon,

and we laughed. Vinnie didn't like it and turned to look at Jimmy but didn't say a thing. One of the old men spat on the ground and said,

115

Richard Hillesley

\- What them lads need is a bloody good war,
and we said,
\- Bet yis.
\- Na.
\- Gan on,
screaming into the cold night air.

Going Down the Road

When I was seventeen, I came south to find a job. I took my belongings in a bag and hitched down the Great North Road with hope and trepidation in my heart. I had a bad time of it and was left to stand by the road throughout the night.

A car picked me up in the afternoon. The driver's face was long and thin. His eyes were sharp and narrow. I wasn't comfortable with him, but I couldn't have told you why. He saw me as a lost soul and I probably saw the same in him, a man in a suit that wasn't going to fit him, stretching in the wrong places, twisting awkwardly round his shoulders. When he stopped at the roadside, he leant across the front seat and said,

- Where are you going?
- South,

I said, and the word had a magic I hadn't heard before.

It was a summer afternoon, warm and wet. The sun came through the swishing clouds, leaving splashes of light and a freshness across the fields. The windscreen wipers clacked and the spray lifted off the tyres of the lorries in front of us. He raced up to the lights of the lorries as we came up behind them, pulling out at the last moment and swinging the car into the outside lane through the spray. It was a relief when the rain began to ease and the sun came out, and the road opened up before us.

Once or twice he glanced at me and I ignored him. The twist of his face made it look like he was peering round a corner. He tried to speak but I preferred to keep a silence. After the sun came out he slowed down a bit, and I began to

117

relax. He pulled up at a Little Chef.

- Hungry?

he asked. I told him I hadn't eaten, and he bought me a roll and a cup of coffee, though it wasn't good and I didn't want him to pay for it. I sat by the window and watched the road go by. He looked at me with a thin-lipped grin and staring eyes. The coffee was hot and wet but tasted all wrong. He had taken a liking to me but something wasn't right about him. I watched the sun play on the glass and listened to his voice though I didn't hear a word he said.

When we got back in the car he began to behave oddly. He turned to look at me, and reached over and put his hand on my knee with a strange gleam in his eye. This wasn't what I was expecting.

- Na,

I said,

- Don't do that.

He took back his hand and acted as if nothing had happened. I looked out the window as the light began to fade, trees and fields and clouds as far as I could see. We drove in silence but the atmosphere changed. I kept my eyes on the road ahead and wondered what would happen next. He veered between the lanes, racing for short periods, swerving behind lorries and slowing dramatically. Each time he did this, he turned to look at me and I stared at the road ahead and the cars floating past. After a while he said,

- Sorry. I didn't mean to be angry,

and the road became more quiet. I wondered what was wrong with him. My bag was on the back seat and I calculated there was no chance of escape. So I kept my eyes on the road, staring into the evening as it came up to meet me, shadows cast by trees which put his face in sharp relief. Just as the road seemed to become more ordinary, he reached across and touched my leg again.

- Ciggie?

he said meaningfully, and took a packet from the glove compartment, tapping it against his leg. He pulled one out, slipped it between his lips, and held the pack towards me.

- Na,

I said, reaching for my own. He held the wheel between his knees while he cupped his hands to strike a match. He took a light and offered it to me, still holding the wheel with his leg as the car began to drift to the left, jerking it back in line just before we hit the kerb. He laughed a small laugh, and said,

- Close thing there.

I stared at the squares of light reflected through the glass in front of me, the arc left by the wipers and the dust on the screen. The sun was low in the sky and the long glow of summer was flowing out across the hills and fields.

- It'll be getting dark soon,

he said, and looked at me.

- Not till half-past nine,

I said, and he slowed down and pulled into the inside lane as we drove up a hill behind a lorry. He drove onto the hard shoulder, stopped the car and switched off the ignition.

- You could stay at my place,

he said, with a hint of a smile on the corner of his lips. Another lorry thundered past and the car shuddered. He put his hand on my knee again.

- Breakfast in the morning and an early start,

he said.

- Na,

I said,

- Don't do that,

and pushed his hand away.

He stared at me angrily, threw the car into gear and pulled out in front of another car, forcing it to swerve out of the way and into the outside lane. I don't think he saw the other car as he stepped on the accelerator and pushed towards the evening sky with an angry determination in his eyes. He evidently wasn't happy, and, ten minutes later, he pulled up on the slip road leading to a country lane, and said,

- You can get out here.

He had promised to drop me at a service station or a junction where I could get a lift, and this was a B-road where there would be little traffic but farm traffic and none of that before morning. I picked up my jacket from the foot well and he shouted,

- Get out,

and as I opened the rear door and reached for my bag on the back seat he yelled across the roof of the car,

- You don't know me.

I looked at him, bemused.

- You've never met me,

he shouted, and jumped into the car and drove away. I sat down at the side of the road and counted my blessings.

There wasn't a hope of a lift on the slip road. I picked up my bag and walked up to the junction, kicking a can as I went. The B-road disappeared into the fields and hedgerows and the fading light on either side of the bridge. I walked down to the side of the carriageway, threw my bag on the grass, and watched the arc of headlights as they drew wild traces along the evening sky, hoping a car might stop for me.

I sat by the hedge and listened to the birds and the hum of the traffic while the sun slipped through the clouds on the horizon. I hadn't been there long when a car pulled up and a girl climbed out. She had a rucksack on her back and didn't seem to have a care. She was urchin-like, thin and bird legged, with a longish skirt and shortish hair, big brown eyes and a street-wise air I could only hope for. The car disappeared along the country road, and she put her bag on the ground next to mine and said,

- Hi,

and looked me over.

- You been waiting long?

- A while,

I said.

- You look tired,

she said, sympathetically.

- Aye,

I said, and flicked a piece of gravel into the grass. We talked about the weather and the road, the sun slipping over the edge of the fields and the drivers of cars who drove straight past us.

- We'll never get a lift here,

I said.

- We will,

she said, but I wasn't too sure. I stood up and walked around. She had a confidence in the road I did not have. I told her about the man with the wandering hands who had dropped me here.

- I've known a few of those,

she said,

- You should try being a girl.

I kicked a pebble into the kerb. She looked at me like I was odd, pushing her hand back through her hair.

- Where you going?

I didn't really know.

- South,

I said.

- Do you know what you're looking for?

- A job.

I said.

- Good luck with that,

she said, scratching the side of her face.

- Work is just another way of starving.

The shadows were deepening and the headlights had begun to penetrate the gloom.

- Come on,

she said,

- Let's hitch together.

She pulled her bag over her shoulder and went to the side of the road. She stuck out her thumb and a lorry stopped a hundred yards further down the road. She ran after it and climbed into the cab and I followed with my bag knocking between my legs. By the time I got there, she was already high in the cab.

- He's only got room for one,

she said, looking down at me.

- See you,

she said, and smiled and waved at me as the lorry pulled away.

The night was coming in. Egg in gristle, the pale moon

turning to cold. I stood on the hard shoulder and watched the traffic. Out of the night the trucks came from the north. Their headlights were slivers of ice, irrevocable and unearthly. They howled like ghosts and sent shivers along my spine. Behind them there was silence and the promise of rain.

Food was what I thought about once the dark crawled in, bringing with it the cold. The lights glimmered in the distance like stars, and hunger filled my belly with sounds. I could see the drivers' faces illuminated by a light in the cab or the glow of a tab on a bottom lip, and felt a sudden and pointless anger towards them, warm in their worlds, cushioned from the night by the rhythms of their motors and the sounds of their radios.

I counted the lorries and I counted the stars. I listened for missing engines and I counted the cats' eyes running down the middle of the road. I ran into the road and a lorry just missed me, blowing his horn as he went.

I waved my arms but the drivers didn't see me. I could see their faces rearing through the gloom, a light in the cab, the radio on, their motors crashing through the dark like space junk through the skies, chasing moonbeams from my shadow, spinning my shadow around my face, taking my shadow away.

I whistled and sang and waited for the echoes to come bouncing back off the road. I sang every song I knew and some I had never heard before. The stars quivered. The gorges opened up beneath me, and the lorries rushed in with a blast of light, falling like meteors through a primeval sky. It was ordained that things would be this way. The night was delivered, and there was nothing I could do but stand there with the cold creeping down my back, waiting for a miracle.

Richard Hillesley

It began to spit with rain and I hid beneath the wings of a bridge with my coat pulled over my head, shivering. I sat down and smoked my last cigarette. I crouched in the cradle of the concrete spans and listened to the wind blowing through the fields behind me, waiting for the morning to come.

At the darkest hour, a blue light came down the road. A police car. Two coppas, faces locked in shadow.
- How long you been here?
one of them said.
- Since dark,
I said,
- Why you asking?
- Break-ins on the industrial estate.
- Not me,
I said.
- Can you prove it?
- Na.

I didn't know where the industrial estate was.
- What's in your bag?
- Nowt.

They stepped out of the car and emptied my bag onto the side of the road, oblivious to my pleas.
- It's raining,
I said, and they laughed. An hour or two later, the sun came slowly, cracking like an egg in a frying pan in a roadside café three junctions down the road, and I stood at the side of the road and read a message written on the side of the bridge, and knew I wasn't the first.
- I know I'm spotty, knackered and stink,
it said,

- but I still want a fucking lift.

A lorry stopped just before dawn, a crack of blue splitting the eastern sky, and I ran like the wind with my bag knocking between my legs. The driver said,
- Where you going?
and I said,
- South.
He shook his head and said,
- I turn off just down the road.
- Na,
I said, and stood between the door and the cab, staring up into his face. I was unable to move. He reached across for my bag.
- Get in.
I sat high in his cab, with my knees up under my chin, shivering, and he looked at me from the corner of his eye.
- Got a job?
- ?
- A job? Do you work?
- Na.
- London?
- Aye.
- Work?
- Aye.
It was a pig lorry.
- A kna this, knowing what a do, a wouldn't eat the buggas, he said.
- Keep em in black holes, stuff 'em with shit, tea leaves, dog ends, piglets, plastic, dead animals, an' cut their throats. It's all gristle and shit.

125

He spat from the window. Light danced on the leaves and fields, rooftops and windscreens. Music on the radio, barely audible above the slamming gears.

- Tab?

- Aye.

- A tak 'em from the prison to the slaughterhouse,
he said, and told me he was thinking of quitting his job to do what I was doing before he grew too old.

He dropped me at a roadside café, a whitewashed shack with a bare lightbulb buzzing above the door. The morning was coming up, pale and fresh beneath a cloudfilled sky, setting the distant trees and chimneys in their place. I lifted my bag and crossed the gravel between the parked lorries and the concrete outhouses. The smell of DERV and the hint of frying bacon floated through the air and a silence hung in the breeze, broken only by the noise of a sign that read BREAKFAST ALL DAY AND NIGHT caught on its creaking hinges, and the ebb and flow of the fading traffic on the road behind me.

I walked on legs that were light and jaunty in their tiredness, grabbing smokes from a machine on the way in. I smiled at the waitress and she turned away with a wilted air that said that she had seen it all before, yet she couldn't have been much older than I was. Her face said,

- What do you want?

and her eyes said,

- Get it over with.

She wore a black skirt with stains on the hem and a plastic apron with a Guinness girder that stretched tight across her hips. Her hair was tied in a distraught bun pinned to the top of her head.

- Breakfast?

she said.

- Chips?
- Aye.
- Beans?
- Aye.
- Coffee?
- Aye.

I sat down at a table by the window and spread myself between the window and the ashtray. It began to rain outside, lightly splattering the glass. I was too tired to care. The rain looked like rain to me and the smoke smelt like smoke. The dust hung in the thick air waiting for a place to settle, like the tensions in the hard struck chords on the radio. My foot tapped, not to the music, but from restlessness. My cigarette flew to my lips and the smoke was restful. It clouded the fraying edges of my nerves. It seeped into the cracks and filled them out.

My coffee span around my cup. It tasted of cardboard and was stiff and dry, but the liquid burnt my tongue and kept me awake. The food came on a cracked plate, an egg with its yolk staring up at me. I ate slowly, prodded a delicate fork into each chip and dipped it into the yolk. The taste and smell lingered on my lips and I listened to the murmur of the drivers talking and the hum of the music on the radio. The noises echoed around the room, crashing plates, the stillflowing tap in the sink, a scraping chair, the drone of a voice on the radio, slithering across the room like an egg yolk sliding down a plug hole.

Richard Hillesley

- *Six o'clock on a sunny morning in London ... an unemployed man set himself on fire outside Downing Street last night ...*

I put my head in my arms and fell asleep. I dreamt of headlights and tyres as big as the moon, rolling down the road, exploding in sheets of light and rain, bridges reaching over the deepest of chasms and rivers of light flowing across the sky.

I saw the lorries and the drivers behind the wheel, deep in their seats and warm in their worlds, wisps of smoke and sound drifting from their cabs, lights and white lines reaching down the road.

All I wanted was a little hope and warmth, and suddenly I was angry and fell on my knees and reached my hands into the night. I spat on their flying wheels and blew on their fading exhausts. I tore the lorries out of the night and flung them back to from where they came and saw them trailing along the frozen edges of the Aurora Borealis, their lights receding until they were pinheads among the frightened stars...

I woke to find the waitress standing over me with a satisfied smile on her face.
- We can't have that in here,
she said.
- What?
I said.
- You can't sleep in here,
she said. So I went outside and yawned and rubbed my eyes, the chill morning wind, fresh after rain, stinging my face. The gravel crunched beneath my feet and the giant tyres scratched the surface of the silver puddles.

Behind me the hanging sky was blue and grey and a sign banged in the wind. I stretched my arms and touched my toes and went to find the toilet. It was a sloping drain leading to a grate below a greening wall and a corrugated roof. There was a tap on the wall. I stooped over it, cupping the cold water in my hands and splashed my face. A driver in blue overalls leant into the corner, pissing in private.
- You going north?
he said over his shoulder.
- Aye.
- I'll take you,
he said, and walked off, hitching up his flies.

From the window of his cab, I watched the light filter through the trees, and the road dissolve beneath me. The pale sun climbed up through the clouds and the bubbling steam from the cooling towers at Ferrybridge. Light touched the scum on the water, the old bridge and the black rails, and we rode over the town in the lorry, motionless.

Richard Hillesley

Thick as Thieves

Outside, the sky is slate coloured and the air is still and lifeless but for the buzz of a fly and the hum of a passing car. The fly hovers over the chair next to the bed. The car turns into the alley below.

The car is the landlord's. I hear him slamming the doors and coming up the stairs. He is spherical and out of breath and the stairs creak beneath him. He puts his nose around the door and sniffs the rent out of the air. He stands in the doorway with his hands in his pockets, on his money and his gut. That is what he thinks about. His money and his gut. The room is damp and cold, and the gas has run out.
- Put some money in it,
he says, as if he cares.
- Aye,
I say, pushing him out and shutting the door behind him. He edges back down the stairs. The stairs are creaking. The hollow planks ache under the strain, and he pushes and pulls at the banister and grunts and splutters as each step rises and falls beneath him.
- The stupid get,
I am thinking,
- I don't have any money to put in it. Hasn't he worked that one out yet?

I am hungry and think only of food. There's a small window that looks out on the yard below, echoes of light on the glass, a bed, a chair and a glass of water, like that room of

Van Gogh's. But this is not the South of France. Here the sun is dirty and inhibited. It swims around corners, moves between shadows and hides in a ditch. The walls and the sheets are drab and lifeless. The carpet has stains on it and the mattress is soft because I am hungry.

I lie on the bed with my stomach hollow and look through the window at the clouds. A flower grows without sunlight against a fence and the smell of food drifts in from the yard next door. I think only of food and try to picture the table and the food. The plates of stew and lumps of bread and cheese are as thick and bright as the sun in Arles. But I can't eat them. I can only breathe them. That's the way it is up here.

I don't know why I came. I should have known better. O'Brien said we would find money and girls. He had a room in this house and a job in a bar. He said he'd lined up a job for me but got himself sacked the day before I arrived, so we're stuck in these rooms without a job and without any money. I should have known it would be like this. He has always been the same. He was like it as a kid. He talks before he thinks, and he doesn't think before he acts. Life is a game of street football, and the goal is the space between the bins and the pullovers scattered along the ground. Nothing lasts and nothing has a consequence. Every job and every girl he meets is the same and the only price he pays is a scrape on the shins. He never sees the mess he leaves behind.

In the morning, we go to the factory to look for a job. The factory is on the industrial estate and makes dried soup. The kind that comes in packets and sachets and is sold in super-markets.

131

It's a grey day. The sun hangs in the sky like a loose rivet, tying the clouds together. We run through the gate with our jackets over our heads, and go to the reception, a room filled with dim echoes and scraping shoes. O'Brien slouches on a chair, and I thumb the rough edge of a matchbox. The clock on the wall ticks loudly. A door opens. A secretary comes in, and O'Brien stands stiffly.

- This way, please.

The man at the desk is bored and irritable.

- Name?

- O'Brien.

The man peers at him over the tops of his glasses. He has thin lips and a weak chin, chews his teeth but doesn't smile.

- Surname?

- That is my surname.

- Brian?

- O'Brien.

- Oh.

- B.

- Ah.

- Temporary?

- Aye,

says O'Brien, but I take a permanent job because the money's better. O'Brien slumps on a chair with his hair falling apart, smoking a cigarette. A chargehand comes in and says,

- Put that out,

and leads him into the factory.

I am left staring at the wall until an old man comes in and tells me to follow him. He has one of those faces that has seen life from the wrong angles and doesn't like it. He has worked for the company since he left school and soup runs through

his veins. He leads me to a room with a projector and a screen, but he loses his fingers in the dark.
- Bugga,
he says,
- I never get these things right, but you get the idea.
- ?
- You get work and you get paid,
he says,
- It isn't like it used to be when you knew who the boss was and the boss knew who you were, and he took care of you because he knew you would work harder for him.
- Was it really like that?
I say.
- No,
he says,
- but it was better than it is now.
- ?
- . . . it's a job,
he says, and I laugh.
- You should be glad you've got a job, lad,
he says.
- Aye,
I say, and he sends me to work in the warehouse with Syd.

I like Syd. His hair flops over his face and he doesn't belong where he is. He should be picking pockets in a scratchy jacket and a top hat in a street of Dickens, not working in a factory where no-one gives him any respect or the prospect of a decent wage. He has a pockmarked chin and a lopsided grin and a face that says,
- Who? Me?

before you think of asking. It is something in the way he carries himself, the lift of his eyebrow, the knowing look, like he knows something about you you don't know yourself. He wears the look of someone who has picked your pocket and has got away with it. He knows his job better than the bosses do. He knows his way round the factory and every dark corner of the job. Our job is to be unseen when we are not needed, and to be seen when we are, to stay out of range of the chargehand when he loses his rag, and to do nothing the rest of the time.

- No-one knows what is going on, and no-one really cares, he says,
- All they know is they are the farmers and we are the stock. They milk us and fleece us until we are gristle and bone, and as long as we know our place and the money's coming in, nobody cares about us.

The warehouse is wide and high and the doors cast shadows across the floor. Our job is to fill the vans and lorries that wait in the yard. The chargehand sits in a shed with a Pirelli calendar and a clerk. The orders come in and he writes up the worksheets on a clipboard and shouts at the clerk.

We take the worksheet and run through the alleys between the shelves. Syd races up ladders, clings to the shelves, swings from the girders and flings boxes at me. I stack them on the pallets, and Charlie swings the forklift and the pallets into the yard. Charlie has a tattoo of a snake up his leg, and his smile is upside down. He takes away the pallets without a word.

- That's it,
says Syd. We sit on a box behind the chargehand's shed and smoke a tab to pass the time. Inside the shed the chargehand

fills a kettle, drinks a cup of tea and talks on the phone. He shouts at the drivers and bullies the clerk, puts his feet on the desk and reads his paper. The phone rings, and he comes out.
- You,
he shouts, and we leap into action, running up the aisle, lurching, lifting and throwing boxes. Another pallet to fill. The ones we filled earlier are still at the gate.
- They go tomorrow,
Syd tells me.
- So why the hurry?
- Catch this one,
he says, up a ladder, leaning one-legged into a stack of shelves, throwing boxes at me.
- Why the hurry?
- Time and motion,
he says,
- We move, and he times us. When we have a job we have to run. When there's nothing to do we stay out of sight.
- That makes no sense.
- None of it makes sense. It's a job,
he says,
- The art of this job is to do nothing creatively. It's as simple and as complicated as that.
- So what do we do with the rest of our time?
- Sweep the floor,
he says. The floor is always swept. Syd is a master at wasting his time. He can sleep standing up with his broom in his hand, sweeping piles of dust into tidy piles of dust. He hides his paper inside his shirt and reads it upside-down. I sneak a book into the tops of my trousers, climb up behind the boxes next to the roof, and read.

I meet a man up there. He has a broken nose, hooked out of shape by a blunt object in the past. He is curled into his overalls, cap on his head. He is asleep and I tap him on the shoulder.

- Who are you?

I say.

Eyes wide, he starts. With the back of his hand, he wipes away the sleep. He gets up and runs over the boxes and falls flat on his face. His cap falls off.

- Alright,

he says,

- You got me.

I pick up his cap and give it back to him.

- It's alright,

I say,

- I wasn't after you.

He peers over the boxes and puts his finger to his lips.

- Shush, will yis? I'm the same as you.

- Playing hookey?

I say. I know what I am doing.

- Na,

he says,

- I'm doing overtime. I'm on the other shift. I come up here and no-one sees me. I clock off at ten. I get four hours overtime like that.

I whistle.

- How's that?

- I don't go home at the end of the shift. I climb up here and come out four hours later. Twenty more hours a week. Good, eh?

- Aye,

I say.

- Watch this,

he says. He leads me patiently across the stacks, and then, lying down, so as to be hidden from the ground, he points among the rafters close to our heads.

- Nests,

he says, and we sit among the boxes and marvel at the birds in the rafters. His name is Leon. He has bright eyes and a slack jaw, teeth crossed like two sticks under the hook of his nose. Once upon a time someone has hit him really hard. I promise I will see him again and he lurches out silently, slowly, to clock off and go home to bed.

- See you do, lad,

he says. And I say I will.

We go to the canteen for the tea break. O'Brien comes in in a hairnet and facemask pulled down under his chin. I haven't seen him since the morning. He asks about my job and I tell him the worst part is trying to look busy. He has a cup of tea but he barely has time to put it to his lips when a supervisor comes in. She stands and claps her hands and he takes a sip and goes back to work, and I can see he isn't liking his job.

We follow him across the yard and Syd takes me into the factory, past men in hairnets who shovel vegetables and bits of animals into vats and troughs and ovens and dryers. The pipes hiss and blow. The engines smoke and pant. Steam rises through the grates, and powdered soup flows out the other end, packed into packets and sachets by lines of women who work in a flurry of hands and hairnets and facemasks. The soup comes down from hoppers in the roof and is filtered along the lines. The lines clack and whirr and no-one has time to stop or think or breathe until a hopper runs empty and a line is stalled. The hoppers are fed from above. The women are on piecework and a stopped line means less soup and less money, and they yell at the roof until someone clanks the machinery back into action, and the soup begins to flow. As one line starts, another one stops, and the yelling never stops.

At the end of the lines is a flight of steps that leads to the floor upstairs. At the top of the stairs is a desk and a plate glass window. Behind the desk is a supervisor. Behind the window is a long dark room. This is where O'Brien works. He is dressed in white overalls, a white hairnet, a facemask and plastic boots. He pushes a wooden wheelbarrow and carries a wooden shovel between the rows of hoppers that feed the lines below.

He shovels soup from the barrow into the hoppers, and as one hopper fills another one empties, and the supervisor points and shouts at him, and the women yell below. He jumps from hopper to hopper with his shovel and his barrow, adrift in a cloud of soup. He runs and coughs between the hoppers, floating on waves of powdered soup, dehydrated peas and dessicated chicken bones. And the yelling never stops.

I knock on the window and wave at him. He looks up and wipes his face with the back of his hand, and doesn't wave back.

I don't see him again till the end of the day. He comes to my room and he isn't happy. Soup has seeped into the cracks of his being. The air he breathes tastes and smells of soup. He has tried soap and water but the smell stays on his body. I try to tell him it's just as bad for me. They work me like a dog. Syd is a bully. My back is sore and my legs are hurting. But he's inconsolable. He hasn't eaten all day. I have a packet of soup I hid in my pocket at work.

- I can make some soup,

I say, and he looks at me.

- I wouldn't eat that,

he says. I empty the packet into the pan, and light the gas.

- Why not?

I am just as hungry as he is.

- I spit in it,

he says, and laughs. Not so much a laugh as a cackle. He looks slightly desperate and shuffles back to his room. I wait until he's gone, and eat it anyway. If we were old and wise, we'd do this differently, but we're young and open to life, whatever it brings, and walk straight into things.

Wednesday lunch time, and the chargehand and his clerk are in the canteen. I sweep the floor and lean on the broom. I stop and look around. There is no-one about. I sweep a few gentle strokes around a corner, and lean against a box. I sit a while, wipe my face and cup my chin in my hands. I have an itch and scratch my thigh and settle down again. Music blows in on the wind and then a voice.

- You,

someone shouts,

- Come here. I've got a job for you.

I don't know who he is. He is thin and wiry and has a sloping walk, like he's leaning back to reach something on the floor behind him.

- Fill that van,

he says, pointing at a Transit van he has reversed up to the gates,

- Put those boxes in it.

I do as I'm told, reassured by the presence of Syd, who has turned up out of nowhere.

- Quick,

says Syd, grinning as he goes, and we fill the van to the brim. When it's filled Syd and the man go into a huddle, and he drives the van away. I don't think about it until Syd takes me aside an hour or two later and gives me some notes.

- Your bonus,

he says, and winks. I think about arguing with him, but I need the money.

When evening comes it blows in with the birds. Crackle of sunlight along the ends of the houses. Flyposters with a pot of glue, running under the arches. The blowing of leaves. I have money and I go to O'Brien's room to drag him out to the pub. I think he'll be pleased, but he's almost resentful.

The pub is dust and smoke. We eat and drink. The band is minimalist and loud. Crashing drums and angry chords like wrecking balls in a breaker's yard. Two lasses across the room look our way. We talk to them. One is up for it, but the other isn't. O'Brien's in too much of a hurry.

- Gis a kiss, pet,

he says. She's definitely not up for it.

- Pissoff,

she says, and I nudge him to shut him up. She takes her friend with her, and we are left with no-one to talk to.

I'm not happy with him. We have to listen to ourselves and the band. We talk about music and fashion and how they have always let us down, giving us the illusion of change, one hairstyle at a time. We fall for it and nothing changes. We live in dreams, all dressed up and nowhere to go, while our dreams are ripped away. And the girls don't want to know us because we are out of sorts with the world.

When we leave the pub we go back to our rooms by the light of the street lamps and the whirling stars. Daylight is becoming a mystery to me. I find the landlord in my room. It isn't the first time.
- Hey,
I say,
- You can't come in here.
- I'm here,
he says,
- Where's my rent?
We've already had that conversation and he knows I'm not paid until Friday.
- It's not Friday yet,
I say.
- I think you've had some girls in here,
he says.
- That's ridiculous. Nobody's been in here but me and you, and you're not supposed to be in here.
He doesn't see it that way.
- It's my room and I make the rules, and the rules are that you can't bring anybody in here.
- I haven't brought anybody in here, and you couldn't stop me anyway.
I look around, and it's obvious he's been looking through my stuff. I throw a towel at the door as he leaves. He is not a farmer, and I am not his cow.

Friday morning I'm in the warehouse with time to kill and

I go to look for Leon in his hiding place among the boxes.

- You want a break?

he says.

- Aye.

- Follow me,

he says, and points up at the rafters.

I follow him. Slowly we climb over the stacks, stopping and bending our heads at the sound of voices, ducking until we reach the place he indicates. There behind the stacks is a door.

- Should be locked,

he says,

- but it never is. There's a padlock on it, but it's useless.

We climb down. The door opens and creaks noisily. I am startled by the daylight and the fresh cold air. There's a disused rail siding and a platform behind the factory.

We run up a steep embankment into an alley. The city is lonely. The morning sun comes in like a stranger, rapping and knocking on doors, wrapped in a steep coat and a long scarf, looking for company and hoping for more.

Leon walks ahead of me, his life written into his face. We go into a café, dripping like a steam engine, condensation on the window.

The man at the counter wipes his nose on the back of his hand and we sit in a corner and stare out the window. Leon has a theory about work, pouts his lips, sucks at the air. Cup tipped to a lip.

 - It's all wrong, the way we work,

he says,

- When you're young and you need money, you get paid nowt. When you get older and you don't need money, they give you a pay rise just for being old. It should be the other way round.

I laugh.

- I mean it,

he says,

- They should pay us more when we're young, and less when we get older.

I stare into my cup of tea. I like his logic, like looking down a telescope from the wrong end. The world is smaller, but perfectly formed.

- They should pay themselves less,

I say,

- and pay us more. Then we'd have a reason to work for them.

The sky clashes above us, and the rain falls as we leave the café, our jackets over our heads, and we go back to work.

Leon hides among the boxes, and I pick up a broom. The grey light pours in through the warehouse doors. I dust and scrape. And still there is no work to do. I watch the clock and tidy the boxes. No orders come in so I go to the toilet. On the wall of the cubicle above the seat someone has scribbled WORK IS HELL in a ragged hand. I look at it as I sit there, staring into the abyss and killing time. A chain is pulled and the world is flushed away, flows around the bowl, gushes through the pipes, rushes down the drains.

There's a yell and I stumble back into the light. It's the chargehand and he has a stick in his hand. He's running through the corridors, waving his stick and chasing Leon, who has his arms around his head as he runs. Leon's game is up, and he has lost his overtime and his job.

We make it through to Friday afternoon, when our pay

comes round. I'm in the warehouse with my pay packet in my hand when O'Brien walks in, throwing his overalls and hairnet onto the floor behind him.

- I'm leaving,

he says,

- See you later,

and he turns and walks out. I think about it for half a minute, stop and look around. There isn't much to stay for. I walk out, chucking my overalls onto the boxes as I go. There he is, walking up the street.

- Wait on,

I say as I catch up with him, the wind whirling around our heads. This part of the city is like a graveyard after years of abandonment by government, barred windows, closed shops. We go to the house and up to O'Brien's room and he makes a cup of tea.

- That's it,

I say.

- Aye. Sometimes you have to realise the bastards are out to get you,

he says,

- and you have to find a way to get back at them.

I am in my room and sitting on my bed. The sun at evening has one foot in the gutter, wears a thin jacket and ragged trousers, comes sneaking round corners like a small-time thief, drifts into the street with a hole in its shoes, lights on the bins and sniffs the air, slips in through the opened window. The landlord wheezes and pops as he climbs the stairs. I meet him at the door, and he wants his rent.

- I won't have your money till tomorrow,

I say, though I have my pay in my pocket. He puts his hands on his gut.

- Get it,

he says.

- I can't,

I say,

- I'll give it you tomorrow.

He doesn't like that, but there's nothing he can do. In a world like this, where everyone is looking out for themselves, we are all the losers. I'd like to tell him that, but he wouldn't understand. I wait until dark, pack up my things and join O'Brien in the street. The moon slips through the clouds and watches over us as we steal away through the night, as free as birds and thick as thieves.

Richard Hillesley

Ragtime Millionaire

A train rattles over the Bridges. A sparrow nests in a crack in a wall between the high old grey old bridges and the public lavatory, which has an open gutter with a red brick surround. The posters look absurd, patches of blue sky and massive letters superimposed on a landscape of asymmetric desolation. Two lads are coming down the street, playing the blues.

- Shillin', lad?

one says. He grabs me by the sleeve, unshaven, standing on the step, a dirt streak on his brow. He is small and lean. A bottle hangs out of his pocket, a beat-up guitar and a trilby hat.

- A haven't any.

  He doesn't give up that easy.

- Haway, lad. Forra cuppa tea.

I pull away.

- Na.

  String and bone fingers on my arm, my elbow in a clamp.

- Slept rough, an' a was mugged.

- Mugged?

- Aye. See this.

  He bends down to show me a lump on his head.

- Feel that . . .

- . . . an' Spit was nearly killed.

  He pulls Spit into the picture. Spit has three layers of coat on his upper body and a rag wrapped around his wrist. He is unsteady and out of focus.

- Na.

- Show 'im, Spit.

   I give him a few quid. It's all I have. He's still holding me,
and he's holding Spit who looks like he'd fall over otherwise.

- Show 'im, Spit.

- Na.

- Prove a dinnat tell lies.

   Spit unties the rag, shows a black clotted gash.

- That's terrible,

I say,

- it'll get worse with that on it. Get it to a hospital.

- Na,

he says,

- A kna doctors, an' a dinnat trust 'em.

   His marra grabs me by the sleeve.

- Yis have a tab, lad?

- Not that a can spare.

- Haway, man?

- Hey, man, what yis like?

- Gis another one for the lad,

he says,

- an' we'll play yis a song.

   You can smell the smoke and the drink on his breath, but
he does a perfect Huddie Ledbetter and plays the blues just
like the records. He sings every hiss and pop and scratch in
perfect syncopation with the 78s and throws his voice like
he's playing three streets away or at the bottom of an empty
swimming pool, stopping every few bars to lift the bottle to
his lips.

- *Everybody's gonna eat my dust,*

he sings,

- *and I ain't gonna make a fuss.*

Richard Hillesley

And Spit plays along. He's back on his feet and howls and blows on the mouth harp in his bandaged hand, just like Jazz Gillum, and follows the wind down the street, smoking and drinking and wailing into the smoke filled air, the crochets and quavers doing splits and pirouettes through the crumbling arc of a Jarrow sunset.

The town and the yards subside. The broken ships and cranes collide with the falling sun. A gull slides through the wind, rocks and wheels and rows. All the works of man are temporary or else unreal.

They stop to light a cigarette.

- *All you little people take your hats off to me,*
he sings,
- *Because I'm a ragtime millionaire.*

Hanging on the Wire

Clearing out his drawers, on his eightieth birthday, for the move downstairs, I found an address on a yellowing scrap of paper: a place in Germany.
- A met him on Christmas Day in France,
he said,
- A probably killed 'im the next day.

He shuffled towards the clouded window, and looked out over the garden he'd known all his life. There wasn't much to it. A croft for the pigeons, a few greens and spuds and an ageing Andersen shelter he still used as a shed. He was born in the front room of the house, and grew up in the bedroom over the coal shed. As a child he ran across the space between the outside toilet and the back door and the image and the emotion had stayed with him, the laughter in his eyes, the bare feet on the tiles and the scrapes on his knees as he ran through the snow.

The scrap of paper went on the fire. I wish I had asked him more but he wouldn't have been forthcoming. He never said much about the war, except in riddles and one-liners.

- It was rat against rat,
he said.
- A was the only one a went with who came back,
he said.
- We put our hands over the top, hoping to be shot and sent home,
he said.
- We should have shot the ones who sent us there,

he said.

- Hey, Tommy.
   Silence.
- Tommy.
   Silence.
- Why are we shooting at each other?
   He didn't know why they were shooting at each other.
- Tommy, why do you want to kill me?
   He knew the answer to that one. Boredom and fear.
- Hey, Tommy.
   A starlit night, snow on the ground. A flare went up. If a don't shoot you, you might shoot me. There were bodies on the wire from an attack a few weeks before, but the cold brought with it a strange sense of peace. The night was still. The earth was hard and crisp and his boots weren't good, but he preferred the cold and the frost to the mud that had gone before. It had rained for months, and the rain had soaked into everything, covering the duck boards and forcing them to wade ankle-deep in water.

   They said it was quiet on this part of the front, but still they lost a few to snipers and shells. He was on a fire step in the trench looking out across the black and white moonscape of the land between the trenches, on the spot where Jimmy Byrne had fallen to a sniper a few nights before. It had been quiet and still. A few guns had gone off to the north. One rifle shot and Jimmy had fallen in the trench, the life taken out of him. He saw him fall to the ground and ran to help him. His dead eyes stared back at him and he shook the lifeless body, but there was no response.

   The unit had been ordered up the line two days before,

whizz-bangs falling out of the sky without a reason. A shell fell among the company as they tramped along the road, miles behind the lines, scattering limbs and horse flesh, and they had marched on regardless, and left their friends, men and horses, to die in the ditches. He hadn't heard the shell that took them until it landed. It came out of nowhere, throwing mud and blood through the shocked air. He had broken step to run among the wounded, but the officers had pushed him back into line.

- Bastards,

he said, but Jimmy said,

- No,

and pulled him back like he had a premonition. Jimmy was his friend. But he didn't know what to think or say when he died.

- Hard luck,

he said, like it was a small setback Jimmy would overcome. He stared into the dark and a coldness ran through him, but he was resigned to it. Bullets and shells picked their targets out of the sky, and couldn't be dodged. Survival was a matter of luck, and you couldn't bring the dead back to life. Tomorrow's bullet might be his, and he woke every morning surprised he was still alive. He stood in his boots in the trench, pulled up the laces and looked out at the sun creasing the sky across the frozen mud. He found a consolation in the alien colours of the sunrise and the cold breath of the wind on his face. He looked at the mist curling through the wire across the trenches and found a glimmer of hope in the resilience of a rat scurrying across a shell-hole or a weed springing through a dead man's ribs. Life went on, in the vagaries and trajectories of the new life springing out of the old, breaking out against the odds where it did not belong. It was better than giving up. In the beginning he blamed the Germans. After a while he blamed the war. In the end he blamed the ones who sent them there.

What were the causes of the Great War? Exams I didn't work for, sitting at a desk, scratching words on paper, as if I knew what they were fighting for, as if they knew themselves. The King was cousin to the Kaiser who was cousin to the Czar. Death came wrapped in a flag. Their bodies are still hanging on the wire.

He went because he went. There wasn't a choice. War was abstract and righteous, promising him death or glory by Christmas, and death wasn't real. His mother had wanted him to stay behind, but he hadn't listened to her. He went to the recruitment office with Geoff the day war broke out. They didn't question why they were there.

He knew Geoff all his life. They played together when they were kids and had shared the first banana either of them ever saw. They won it for jumping into the canal to save a small child from drowning on their way to school.

They had been walking to school along the canal when one of them tripped and they fell in the water. They were late for school and made up the story about jumping into the canal to save a child to save themselves from a beating.

They were called out in assembly the next morning and the headmaster gave them a banana for their bravery, the first banana they had seen. That was in 1906. He was ten years old.

At the recruiting office, they were weighed and measured and asked for their names and dates of birth. They came out with their chests stuck out and their heads held high, and the girls cheered them off to war. It was as simple as saving a child from drowning in the canal.

What were the causes of The Great War? The sun was stained with the blood of our fathers and their fathers before them. They scaled the tips and coughed up the dust on their lungs. Death came wrapped in a flag. Their bodies are still hanging on the wire.

- Hey, Tommy.

The German in the trench opposite wasn't giving up. He had done this every night for over a week, shouting greetings and insults. He spoke good English and laughed a lot. Said he'd worked in England before the war. The lads called him The Kaiser, and some took a liking to him. It was only talk and talk didn't hurt a soul, and they knew by now that the German lads bled and died just like them. Others saw it as an invitation to take potshots at him, but they never hit him. And some, like the captain, took it personally. He was going to get him.

The night before Christmas Eve the captain came along the trench, waving his pistol, and said,

- Come on, lad, You're with me.

It was planned and he was expecting it, but he didn't want to go. The moon was out, and the light glinted on the frost. He didn't like the captain, and he didn't like the plan. Not that it was much of a plan. The idea was to get close enough to hear the Kaiser shouting, and kill him.

Nobody liked the captain, because he put his men at risk and gave them punishments they didn't deserve. He was a leader of men and a winner of medals, but the men knew him for what he was, a fool who put their lives in danger and didn't care whether they lived or died. Night patrols were a chance to show how reckless he could be. He took risks for himself and for those who went on patrol with him, and didn't seem to care how many men were killed to prove how brave he could be. He had been lucky so far and had come out alive, unlike some who had gone with him. Smithson had become a hero because of him, and he was dead. The captain had led three of them into a machine gun nest. Smithson smelt a rat and went the opposite way. He killed the Germans, saving the captain and the others, but was killed himself. He was given the Military Medal, but he was dead by then. There were no heroes in this war. Only the dead and the living.

For the captain it was just a game. He didn't seem to care that his men were dying for no good reason. Or maybe that was what he wanted. He showed no remorse or pity. Crawling through the wire was exciting, diving into shell holes, dodging bullets and springing surprises on German patrols, bringing back prisoners, and coming out alive when all around him died. No-one liked war as much as he liked war, but it was never him who paid the price.

What were the causes of The Great War? White feathers and doffed caps. The boys who shot the boys who shot the boys. Over the top and into the fire. Come the evening the sky is a washed out rag and the fields are awash with tears. Death comes wrapped in a flag. The bodies are still hanging on the wire.

He was given a white feather when he was home on leave. He went home straight from the line, and his uniform crawled with lice. His mother made him strip in the yard before he went in the house. He went straight into the tin bath on the kitchen floor. She put his uniform in the wash and changed him into normal clothes, and he went out for the evening dressed in civvies. A girl he once knew saw him out of uniform and made the wrong assumption and gave him a white feather, and a crowd gathered round him.

He tried to tell them but they wouldn't listen, and a fight broke out. One of them made to hit him, and he beat him up until Lottie dragged him off. She knew the truth and told them loudly, and they were a bit ashamed, but it troubled him anyway, because truth was thin-skinned and what people thought they knew was wrong. They knew what they knew, and were proud in their ignorance. While he was at the front, he sent Lottie a card every week that said no more than,
- To Lottie from Dick,

He was alive and that was all she needed to know. Love was strong and so was she, and that was all he knew. She would have liked him to say more, but words wouldn't have changed a thing.

Returning to France after the trip home, he bumped into a pal at King's Cross. They went for a quick drink, missed the train and got back to France a day late. He was given Field Punishment Number One. For three hours a day, he was hung out to dry, lashed to a post with his arms open wide, crucified. He took it as it came, but he hated the captain after that. He was always in trouble for not quite following the rules, but he kept his self belief and his pride intact. It made him hard as nails, and he was ready to jump with his fists at anyone who challenged him.

What were the causes of the Great War? The boys who shot the boys who shot the boys. Over the top and into the fire. Gavrilo

Richard Hillesley

Princip shot Arch Duke Ferdinand. Revenge came wrapped in a flag.
Their bodies are still hanging on the wire.

The captain led them over the fire step, just the three of
them, the captain, him and Geoff, rifles in hands, balaclavas
pulled over their heads and mud on their faces. They crawled
across no-man's land, ducking from shell hole to shell hole. It
was a cold starlit night and the ground was hard and crisp
beneath them. They snaked across the gravelled mud,
knowing there might be Germans crawling out there, too,
between the skulls and the shrapnel, using shell holes as
places to hide. He put his hand on something. A turnip or a
swede still sitting there in this field of bones. In years to come
this farmer's field would yield a harvest of blood and guts
among the ladies' smock and grass and cuckoospit, death and
rust and ghosts. A flare went up, and lit the ground all
around. The air was shocked. But the Germans weren't
shooting. They had raised Christmas trees lit with candles all
along the trenches. They were singing carols. *Stille Nacht,*
heilige Nacht. He knew that tune. It had bled its way through
his bones from infancy. Snow on the houses. Snow in the
street where he lived. Snow in the yard at night.

What were the causes of the Great War? Treaties and
intransigence. Mischance and fear. Zeppelins in the sky.
Dreadnoughts over the waves. Revenge came wrapped in a flag.
Their bodies are still hanging on the wire.

- Merry Christmas, Tommy.
   The night was crisp and cold. A rat scurried past his face.
The voices of the trench choir were loud and keen. *Stille Nacht,*

heilige Nacht. Rising through the air, rough at the edges, falling through the night. He lay still on the ground, slivers of ice and a shiver in his bones. He didn't want to give himself away, clinging to his rifle, splayed across the frozen mud in a shell hole like a shot pigeon, his breath making shapes in the air.

The singing slid down the side of the sky, falling into silence. *Stille Nacht, heilige Nacht.* And a lone baritone rose from the British trenches, soaring above the silence like a hawk on the wind, balancing on air. Both sides were playing this game. Peace was breaking out.

- Hey, Tommy.

The Kaiser rose out of the trenches. He was shocked to see him, loud hailer in hand, standing above the rim of the trench, only twenty or thirty feet away, tall and proud against the sky, waving towards the British trenches. He was out in the open, and he wasn't alone. Others were running up and down the line, making friendly noises. It was almost as though the war was over. The captain whispered,

- Shoot him,

but the butt of the rifle was cold in his hands and he couldn't bring himself to pull the trigger.

- A can't,

he said, and laid the rifle down. He was thinking about Lottie as he lay with his face in the ice and the mud, and he wasn't thinking about the captain.

- Fire that bloody thing,

the captain hissed, and pointed his pistol at his head.

- A can't.

- I'm going to have you for this,

the captain said, and looked him in the eye, shaking with rage

157

and the pistol trembling in his hand, But Geoff crawled up behind him and said to the captain,
- If you shoot him, a'll shoot you.

The captain rolled over and hissed,
- You're both on a charge when we get back,

Shot at dawn, blindfolded and tied to a post. No different to going over the top and not knowing where the next bullet was coming from.

The captain pointed the pistol between his eyes.
- shoot him,

he said. And suddenly the sky exploded. Both sides were sending flares and fire crackers into the clouds, lighting up the ground for miles around. A cheer went up from the German trenches, and an echo came back from their own. Peace was breaking out.
- A can't,

he said. The pistol dropped from the captain's hand and he slumped to the ground. Geoff had shot him. They lay in silence for a moment and looked at each other, before snaking back slowly across the broken ground. The moon came out from behind a cloud. They were nearly back at the trenches before either of them said a thing. Men had emerged into no-man's land and were standing between the wire and the shell holes, and officers were wandering among them, trying to send them back. For a moment war had lost its meaning and fear was gone. They reported the captain missing but little more was said.

On Christmas Day, the men casually drifted out across no-man's land, as if the war was over, and gave each other addresses on scraps of paper and promised to meet again, but within a week or two the fighting resumed and many of them lay dead and dying across the turnip field. Geoff was killed in an attack on the Messines Ridge three years later, and the captain's body sank into the shell hole where he had fallen and was never seen again.

He sat in front of the fire, smoked his pipe and stared into the coals. I asked him about the war, and he looked at me and said,
- A didn't like it much,
and spat into the flames.

Richard Hillesley

Stilled in the Landscape

We pitched our tent in the glow of evening on the grass by
the small wooden pier where the fishing skiffs were tied. The
hotel was on its own in a scatter of trees in a landscape of
peat-bog and moor. The hunters gathered in the bar in
camouflage and Barbour, dressed for the kill, connoisseurs of
loud talk and whisky. A fire in the corner. A chill in the glass.
- We do it for the kill,
one of them said,
- and the thrill of the chase.

Clouds of light and shade spilled out of the high rivers and
the streams that flowed down from the hills and filled the
lochan with trout and Arctic char. Most of the visitors came
to fish. One or two were still on boats on the water as the sun
went down. They had rods and nets on sticks and bait and
food, and paid for the right to fish.

To fish was to imagine the impossible while doing nothing, to dream of rods and flies and the smell of the water, the
stirring of the flies on the surface and the ripple of life among
the reeds and the grasses. The trick was to trick the fish into
hooking themselves.

The sun went down over the hills and we slept in our tent
by the water. The night was cool and bright, and the light on
the water reflected the lights of the stars back at the sky.

The next morning we went up on the moor and lay in the
grasses and watched the gillies in Land Rovers pick out a stag
on their walkie-talkies. The deer merged with the bracken,
and stared with eyes like pools of water. The birds, startled,

rose into the safety above.

- The deer can smell the guns,

one of them said,

- They can sense the crackle of the radios in the air.

The stag was upright and stiff in the wind. He was old and his place in the rut was lost but he had grace and attitude. He was alone in the grasses, upwind of the gillies who pushed him away from where he wanted to be. The wind was soft and bright and his nose was in the air.

The hunters spent the morning in the bar. The gillies led them into the hills and away from the stag. Their scent drifted across the moor. The stag was stilled in the landscape, where he could not run.

- It's the tracking I love,

one of them said,

- and the scent of the deer.

The gillies led them up the back of the wind, sniffing the spoor and scratching the scent out of the soil and the grasses. We could see their shadows as they went over the rise of a hill and along a spur, walking away from the deer, which they could not see. They followed a trail that took them over the dip of a hill and out of our sight, stepping on flat stones over a stream, and back along the ridge to come within sight of the stag.

They lay on the ground between the shadows of the clouds and the murmur of the streams. The blast was harsh and split the bone. There were two shots. One from the hunter, and one from the gillie at his side.

- Just to be sure.

the gillie said later, though the stag ran for twenty feet or more before he fell to the ground.

Richard Hillesley

The hunter closed in on the stag to pose for pictures. He knelt in his hat on one knee. The guts of the stag were left on the ground for wild cat or fox, and a gillie dragged its carcass onto the back of a Land Rover, to be taken down the hill for antlers and venison. And the hunters went to the bar to brag and drink. The thrill of the chase and the kill, and the clash of glass upon glass, eyes like puddles of beer.

And we came down from the hills and lay in our tent, a red triangle in the grass. And two of the fishermen drifted in skiffs like Buddhas on the water, rods in the sky. And we dived in the water to explore the pebbles and the reeds and the cool of the water as it ran over our bodies and cleansed our limbs.

A Poet of the Western Shore

Willie plays the fiddle and it's a beautiful thing. On a Saturday evening, when the boats are in and the wind is getting up, he comes into the bar and begins to play. His hands are as big as shovels but he is a sculptor of notes, carving light out of the clouds with a clarity that could charm the birds down from the trees and make hard men weep.
- Look at him,
Loki says,
- He has a jaw like a JCB, yet he plays like an angel.
    And it's true. He can dig roads with his bare hands, but he handles the fiddle like he is playing one of Picasso's guitars. He picks up his bow and the air becomes light. He says little, but he doesn't need to talk. He comes out of the wind and in from the street, never looking for more than a dram and a chance to play, and in the morning he will be gone, nobody knows where to. When he puts his fiddle down, the regulars know the score.
- Buy him a dram,
someone will say, and he will play some more.

    Evening casts a net over the land, the hint of a storm in the offing. Clouds soar over the western coast, and the ferry is tied up in harbour on the other side of the sea, waiting for the weather to clear. Loki's boat is one of four or five up against the quay, a working boat heavy with the smell of the sea, wind pulling at the nets and buoys, the pull of the water tugging at the ropes and ties.
    He is a fisherman, skin creased by the wind, eyes looking

into the distance, a dreamer anchored by the tides. He has the legs and stance of someone who is used to keeping his balance on a moving deck, but he is just as likely to be in the pub with a girl as he is to be at sea.

- I like it,

he says, and who can blame him? To the locals, who have grown up with the nets and creels wrapped around their toes, fishing is a way of life and they have no choice, but to Loki it's an escape. He goes to sea to be free. He relishes the sea and its moods. He can do the things you need to do on a boat. He can fix an engine and ride a storm, but he likes the pub and the girls too much. During the best days of summer when he should be bringing in cash to cover the storms of winter, he is in the pub and putting things off.

- The fish can wait,

he says,

- We can catch them another day.

But it doesn't work like that, and he knows it. There is something in the air of the place. He is riding the wild surf and coming down the wave.

The storm comes in slowly over the sea, lifting the tops of the waves and disturbing the air. A swirl of gulls breaks the silence with shrieks and stabs in the loud wind of evening. Everything responds only to itself. Even the wind carries its own silence, the shouts of kids lost in the hush, the rush of gulls spilling out of the clouds, the clouds swelling out of the sea.

The bar is by the pier. It isn't much of a building but it's the first choice of the fishermen on a Saturday night. The air is thick with talk and smoke. The tables and chairs are hard and spare. The windows are big and wide, and look out onto the pier. Willie plays his fiddle and Loki and Doggie are in the corner with a pint. Doggie is Loki's deckhand. They have had a good week. Loki took the boat to the south of Lewis and filled her up with venison from one of the big estates. The deer were smuggled onto the boat by the gillies. It wasn't legal and it wasn't the kind of work Doggie had signed up for. But the money is enough to keep them afloat for a month or two. The deer were offloaded onto a lorry on a beach at the end of the loch, and the catch has been dispersed among the hotels up and down the coast.

- the biggest catch I ever had,

says Loki.

The wind howls and Donald comes in, as he does every Saturday, red-faced and big-bodied. He drops his bag on the floor, and says he can only stop for one. He says this every week at about this time. His wife is a Free Presbyterian, and she doesn't like him drinking. Every week, on a Saturday when the fishermen are in, he joins the others and it goes too far. He gets home after midnight, drunk, and every week she locks him out. The others chide and tease him for his weakness, but he can't do anything about it. Every week he comes into the bar, and someone says,

- I'll get you a pint, Donald.

and he says,

- No. I can't.

- Why not?

- I can't.

- What's the matter with you?

- I'll get you one anyway.

165

- No.
- Too late.
- Just the one.
- Pint, Donald?
- I have to go.
- Your round.
- She'll kill me.
- She'll be alright. You've only had the one.
- Aye well. Just the one.

But it is never just the one. He drinks until he is unsteady on his legs and staggers home. And his wife locks him out and he bangs on the door, and she leans out the window and tells him she won't have a drunk in her house on the Sabbath. And he has to spend the night on his boat and sleep in the same wet bunk he sleeps in when he is at sea.

- She's got you, Donald,

someone will say, and he'll feel angry with her, but he knows that he's in the wrong. He loves his drink and temptation always gets in the way.

By nightfall there is a shimmer on the edge of the world. A troubled sense of peace. Hints in the wave-tops. The clouds are rushing in. The wind is getting up, and the rain begins to fall. The ferry won't arrive until the early hours when the worst of the storm is over, and the passengers come into the bar to look for shelter from the wind and rain. Most of them are tourists, travelling through the isles with rucksacks and wind in their hair. A few are folk musicians, off to a festival on the other side. And there's a girl with a rucksack who sits next to Doggie, and puts her rucksack on the floor beside him. She has something of the gypsy about her, a wilful sense of

being alive, bright eyes and a knowing innocence. He says,
- Where you going?
and she says,
- Anywhere you're going.

It's a seductive line, and it draws him in. But she doesn't know him the way the locals know him. His jeans are torn. His hair flies at angles. Anger is his energy and he is at odds with the world and everything in it.

Everything about him is a statement and he doesn't care what you think. He has a pet gull for no reason other than no-one else likes it. He raised it from a chick. It has a beady eye and follows him up and down the street, flapping around him like a dog. It is there to look out for him and to annoy the people he doesn't like. In return, he feeds it scraps of fish.

It's hard to know what the gypsy girl sees in him. Maybe it's the defiance in his eyes or the nomad in his soul. But she's talking to him and he's up for it.

Willie sits in the corner in a hat that falls around his face and a pullover that's too big for him. He isn't getting the response he wants so he falls silent for a while, picks up his bow and his fiddle splits the air with a cry like the evening cry of the albatross looking for a mate among the gannets and the skuas of Unst or Sula Sgeir, and someone brings him a dram.

A man in a suit with a cagoule pulled over his jacket, waiting for the ferry and slightly the worse for wear, listens to him play, and says,
- Who is he?
- Willie.
- Yes, but who is he? Where did he learn to play like that?

167

Richard Hillesley

No-one knows where Willie got it from. He plucks it out of the air, and no-one wants to draw lines around it or find a beginning or an end.
- That's amazing,
he keeps saying. And everyone knows it's true.
- that's beautiful,
he says, and someone says,
- Get him a dram.
- I can make him famous,
he says, and Willie puts down his fiddle, lets the silence flow and plays a tune the man will know. Smoking and whistling into the smoke-filled air of the pub he plays a few notes, and stops.
- Get him a dram and he'll play for you,
says Loki, and the man in the suit goes to the bar. When he gets back he says,
- I'm a radio producer,
his tie awry, leaning over Willie with a dram in his hand.
- and I can make him famous.

Willie looks at him, takes a swig from the glass, and leans into his face.
- Fuck off,
he says,
- I'm just a bum.

It isn't personal. It's just the way he is. He doesn't speak to anybody, but to those who have heard him play he is a poet of the western shore. The tunes fall out of the sky and things happen around him while he plays, fights and love affairs, failing dreams and lost romances, and he doesn't see or hear or care what is going on. He plays, and he plays until he wants to play no more.

By midnight, a gale is blowing. The rain is hard, thrashing the windows and the shore, and Donald finds his inner preacher. His god sees the world in black and white and doesn't like the drink or the music.

- But you like Willie's playing,

says Loki.

- Willie's different,

he says.

- And you like a drink,

says Loki.

- I do,

he says, and smiles. He's aware of his doubt and ambivalence but his god is the only god he knows.

- Has she locked you out again, Donald?

says Loki.

- Aye,

says Donald, and smiles into his drink. Maybe it's the storm. Maybe it's the drink, but he gets up and walks out of the pub and goes down to his boat, windswept and sorry. The night is heavy on his shoulders and the wind is blowing him sideways.

Willie picks up his fiddle and plays a jig. It rocks the air, and the gypsy girl wants to dance. Doggie doesn't want her to dance, but she's going to dance anyway. And Willie's in the mood. A man without a home, he knocks on doors and lets himself in. And tonight it's the gypsy girl who spins to his tune. A note touches her heart and lifts her up, his arm bent at the elbow, his seven fingers fretting the strings, his bow stroking the midnight air.

- So it goes,

someone says, and the fiddle sinks into his chin and he strokes the strings of her heart, and she spins between the table-tops while the men stamp and clap. She turns the walls on their side and the floor upside-down. The stars in the night revolve, and the fiddle lights the air and blows the night away.

And the musicians join in. They play and whoop and yell and knock out the rhythm on the tables. And the gypsy girl dances and the floor shakes. And Loki, who isn't a dancer, gets up to dance. He grabs the gypsy girl by the hand, and she spins across the floor.

Doggie doesn't like it. He's jealous but he won't admit it. He feels that Willie and Loki have taken his dream away, though they really haven't. He puts down his glass and slips into the night when he thinks no-one's looking.

Loki doesn't notice that Doggie has left. After a reel or two, he spins back across the floor to sit alone with his pint. He is tapping his feet and lighting a cigarette when he looks up, absentmindedly, and sees Donald through the window, bent into the wind and the rain, rushing up the street.
- Ah no,

he says, grabs his coat, and runs for the door. Donald's wearing a cagoule, pulled tight around his face, his beard sticking out below, and he's carrying an axe in his hand. Loki knows what the axe is for. It's the one he keeps on the boat for cutting away the ropes if the nets or lines are snagged, and for weeks Donald has been threatening to use it to break down his door and let himself in. Everyone laughs and teases him and no-one thinks he will ever do it. But he's got the axe, and he's racing up the street.

Loki chases after him. But he's too far behind him and gets there too late. The door is in shreds and Donald's sitting in his front parlour with his head in his wife's arms, and the wind and the rain are blowing in from the street.

She hadn't locked the door, and Donald's feeling a bit foolish. She has a hint of a smile on her lips and waves Loki out. He is feeling guilty that he has teased Donald and led him into it, and goes back onto the street to head for the pub and finish his pint.

The wind tears at his coat and the rain pours down his neck. But it's not over yet. He has just turned the corner when someone jumps on his back and flings him against the wall, an arm around his neck.
- Hey,
he shouts, and tries to elbow him in the ribs.
- Who's that?
he shouts. It's Doggie and he's angry.
- Leave her alone,
he says.
- Who?'
- Bastard.
- Leave it, Doggie. I'm not after her, and she's not interested in me. She just likes dancing.
There's a stand-off before Doggie lets go of his neck, and says,
- Sorry, man.
And Loki puts his arm around him, and they head back to the pub through the rain, and argue for a while before she comes over and sits beside Doggie and gives him a nudge and a smile.

In the morning the storm is gone, but it has left its traces in the wind and the waves. The sun is timid and fresh, slides around corners, throws splinters of light across the tops of the waves. The air is nervous. Gulls fall through the wind, and the boats in the harbour jangle in the breeze. It's the Sabbath and the shops are shut, and Loki goes to the pub by the pier for the Sunday papers, coughing last night from his lungs and wiping the smoke from his eyes.

The pub hasn't recovered from the night before. Bodies and bottles are scattered around the bar. The ferry has gone, but some have missed it. Willie lies across a chair, his mouth wide open, hat tipped over his face, snoring, and two of the travelling musicians have fallen on their stools against the bar, and another lies on the floor, as if shot, a guitar on the carpet beside him.

Loki wipes his eyes and walks into the light, and sees Doggie running along the pier, and the gypsy girl is running towards him with her arms open wide. His gull flies over their heads, and a mist moves across the water towards the opposite shore.

Lungs

The history master was a gruff man, brow ridged with incredulity, chip-lipped and sardonic. His hair, clipped to a tuft, rode his head like a wave. His words were bare, crisp, and to the point.

- Educate thyself,

he wrote on the board, and turned his thin neck towards the class and looked at us sourly, silently, over the tops of his spectacles, not expecting a response, but demanding one anyway.

- That's what they used to write on the union banners,

he said, pausing for effect before he moved wearily to his chair and sat down, twirling the stick he carried between his fingers, tapping the desk.

- I'm not here to teach you,

he said,

- My job is to keep you off the streets. And your job ...

He removed his spectacles and rubbed the back of his hand across his right eye.

- is to teach yourselves.

It was a haunting performance, and we believed him. He was a piece of living history, grey skin rough at the edges, molluscs on his chin, fossilised in stone, thin lips and hard eyes that had seen everything and knew it, spectacles balanced on the rim of his nose, reflecting squares of thin light from the windows, and hidden at the corner of his mouth a hint of warmth and a smile, though he wouldn't want us to know it. He was supposed to be indifferent. He was supposed to be disdainful. He was supposed to dislike

173

us though none of us believed him. It wasn't difficult to see a sensitivity behind his scorn, a bruised romanticism that surfaced in sudden bitterness or nostalgia in his voice when he talked about the people he believed in, those who had fought for our right to dignity. We had things on a plate, not because it was our right, not through the kindness of others, but because people had fought for it. And we should never forget it.

- You won't know how lucky you are until it's gone,
he would tell us.

On Friday afternoons we had him for two hours. Every week he would pick two kids at random to read out their essays, and we would discuss what they had written. Every week I sat at the back of the class, hidden from view by the kid in front, and copied my essay from the exercise book of a kid in the year above us, who had done the same course the year before. I copied them word for word and was always given lesser marks, which I never understood. But I always had an essay to put on his desk at the end of the afternoon, and he would raise his eyebrows and look at me oddly. Sometimes he almost smiled, and I would feel nervous, thinking he had found me out, but he never did, because he seldom moved from the front of the class. And then, one Friday, as was bound to happen, he called me out to read my essay and I didn't have one to read.

- I don't have it.
- Why not?
- I forgot to pick it up when I left this morning,
was all I could think of to say.
- I left it at home,
I told him as he peered at me over the tops of his spectacles.

- You left it at home, sir?
- Aye, sir.
- Where do you live?
- Sir?
- Where do you live?
- Sunderland Road, sir.
- You can run home and fetch it, then.
- Aye, sir.

He had found me out, and I could feel the smiles of the other kids on my back as I picked up my haversack that had the names of popstars and models written on it in coloured ink, and walked out of the class. Beaten, they thought, and how could I know I wasn't? I ran down the stairs, flying past a teacher who thought about pulling me up, but didn't, along the high walled corridor between the sporting plaques and the faded print of Degas's *Absinthe Drinkers* that lined the wall, and into the school library.

I sat skewiff at a study table under the high windows with the slanting light falling across my books, my pen copying the words of last year's essay, the causes of the First World War, the ritual litany of alliances and assassinations, desperation and stupidity, a world that had become comfortable with its madness, where millions died so that schoolboys could write essays about it.

And the sky outside filled with rain, and the room shook with thunder, and lightning flashed between the clouds, washing flying between the house-ends, puddles forming in the schoolyard, a gardener running towards the bicycle sheds with his jacket pulled over his head. And I had an excuse for taking my time, the storm blowing noisily across the streets, the rain falling through the dark urban sky, as I scribbled carelessly between the margins of my exercise book.

I stuffed my things into my haversack, pen and ink and books, pushed past the librarian in her clumsy gown, carrying a thick pile of books under her crooked arm, and half-walked, half-ran, along the echoing corridor past kids moving between lessons to the big door that led into the school yard. I pushed the door open and shivered in the disturbing shock of cold air, the rush of water from the roof-gutters gurgling in the drains. The rain hit me in the face and stung my eyes, and I stood, shrivelled and flapping like a drowned pigeon, until the water had washed though my hair and down the back of my neck, and I knew the history master would know I had suffered in the cause of his essay. A teacher saw me, stood in the doorway, and shouted,
- What are you doing?
and I said,
- Nothing, sir,
pretending an innocence I did not have.
- Get inside,
he said, and I coughed, and ran through the corridors and up the stairs to the class. I didn't knock as I was supposed to, but threw open the door and stood in the doorway, panting and wet, rain dripping from my hair and blazer. Atkinson stood at the front of the class with his book in his hand, reading aloud, mumbling and uncomfortable. The history master tugged at his elbow, and looked at me, with his eyebrows raised over the rims of his spectacles.
- And did you find your essay?
he said.
- Aye, sir,
I said, pulling the haversack off my back, rummaging for my

essay, the dim words that meant nothing to me, the history that was somehow detached from my everyday problems but at their root. Death wrapped around with flags. Over the top and into the fire like the infantry. I didn't have a chance. I didn't have an excuse. But I did have my essay, and I said,
- It's here, sir.
And I knew that he knew I had pulled it out of the fire, and he didn't know how I had done it. From now on he would watch what I was doing, so I wrote my essays on Thursday nights so I had them for his lessons, but I copied them, every one, from the previous year's exercise book. And still he gave me lesser marks than the year before. So I might as well have written them myself.

That was the winter I began to see Lorraine. We used to nick off school on Tuesday afternoons and go to her sister's place and kiss and fumble with our hands over each other's bodies. I met her at Ann Franklin's house just after Christmas. Our first date we went to see a film at the Tyneside Film Theatre. We were seventeen and shy, walked a knowing distance apart, sat on the train too close, shoulder and thigh touching with an anxious warmth, talked abstractly, our breath forming small clouds of steam, names etched into the condensation running down the window.

It was cold, and we shivered as we touched. I had the beginnings of a cold, a mild soreness at the back of my throat and an itch in the tonsils that I noticed as we walked past the worn stone of St. John's where the starlings swirled around the bare trees in a rush of sound. She turned to me and caught my eye soothingly, and I reached out and offered her my hand as we walked up Grainger Street, and she took it, and squeezed.

We went to a pub to get warm before the film began. I walked in behind her, proud to be with her, noticing the looks she pulled and the glances she gave to me as we walked across the room, conscious of the smell of her hair and the whoosh of her dress. We stood at the bar, trying to catch the attention of the barman, my hand on her shoulder, looking around the room when I caught sight of the history master, sitting in a corner with his wife, looking the other way.

- Ah na. I cannit bear it.
- What's the matter?

Lorraine asked.

- Nothing,

I said. But I curled my legs around behind her and out of his sight, and pulled her to the opposite end of the pub, and we left in a hurry. I was sure he had seen me. He had stood up, pulling on his coat, just as I had gone through the door. But Lorraine smiled and pushed me and said,

- Don't be soft,

and I followed her down the street and threw my arms around her from behind, and lifted her off her feet.

- Get off,

she said. And that might have been that, except that when we sat down to watch the film, I saw the shadowed outline of the history master and his wife being ushered into the seats along the row from us. I buried myself deep in my seat and tried to hide, but he saw me, and shook his head as if I had no right to be there. I said a mute hello across the seats, but he didn't answer. The lights dimmed. The coughing and talking died down, and the titles came up on the screen, a soft film about a blonde-haired acrobat who had run off with an army deserter, ending in a field with a gun, shot up with butterflies, a tracking shot over the landscape and Mozart filling the air.

I don't know why. Maybe it was the dust in the cinema, a hundred damp coats come in from the cold, the used air or the silence and the stiff backs in front of me, but my nose and throat began to itch and I couldn't move, a trickle at first wettening my upper lip and the back of my hand. I used my sleeve and sniffed slowly and silently, but it didn't work. I tried watching the girl in the film, not breathing, or thinking of sex and of Lorraine's fingers when she reached to touch my hand. I felt in my pocket but my handkerchief wasn't there.

And the film was soft and quiet. The girl was shot up with lace and butterflies, and whenever it mattered they walked through a silent landscape to the sound of trees in the wind and the singing birds and my nose. My hand was wet, my lip was wet, and the flood kept on coming. I decided to move but sat rigid between Lorraine and a man in a wideboy suit, who looked at me sideways every time I sniffed. And beyond him was the history master, eyes fixed sternly on the screen. It was a hard decision but I nudged the man in the wideboy suit and said,

- Sorry,

though it wasn't enough. He raised his eyes to the roof, and stood up reluctantly, and I edged my way along the row to the history master who looked at me hard, shaking his head.

- Couldn't you wait?

he said.

- Sorry, sir,

I said, and pushed past his wife, who wouldn't even stand up.

- Sorry,

I said.

179

- Sorry.
- Scuse me.
- Sorry.

Each person I passed sighed and was unwilling to rise. And the heads craned around me and through me. The film had reached a crucial moment and I had missed it, saying sorry and ducking and weaving through the bent bodies and the shoes and the handbags and the half-raised seats, the faces upturned to the light. I held my nose in my hand, scared I might spoil their evening, scared I might cough in their faces. My score was Mozart, the music rising with each footstep I took and the toes I trod on, the piano and the violins soaring as I ran up the aisle, through the curtains and into the light, breaking into the silence. The surprised usher at the door tried to hide the cigarette in her hand, and looked startled, and then indifferent.

I ignored her, my face in my hands, and ran up the stairs to the toilets, stood under the bare lightbulbs, leaning over the trough with my nose between my fingers, and blew, and the light rushed in, and I felt like a man of the First World War crawling out of the dark after so many years, my nose and throat like an opened sluice, the cistern pouring through my gills, disinfectant washing through my consciousness, the music ebbing through the walls. I stood and blew and I blew again. I filled my hands, and washed them in the sink, and went into the cubicle to grab some toilet roll, but all they had was Jeyes paper, hard and sharp, like blowing your nose into a bowl of cornflakes. I thought of Lorraine on her first date with me, and went back because of her, past the usher who looked at me stiffly, down the dark aisle, my eyes unadjusted to the light, wiping my nose with the back of my hand, bumping and pushing myself back along the row of half-lit faces.

- Sorry,

I said.

- Sorry.

- Mind.

- Sorry.

And the man in the wideboy suit said,

- Oh, sit down, will you?

And I sat down, and Lorraine took my hand in hers, and I didn't feel so bad. But my nose kept on running, allergic to the film, to the cinema, and to the man in the wideboy suit, his aftershave and his hair. And each time I blew my nose the Jeyes paper cracked in my hand, and his face creased like an overcoat in the wind, and I couldn't help feeling pleased by the look of disgust he gave me after the lights came up at the end of the film and I pushed past him to go the toilets for another handful of paper.

The history master was in the foyer waiting for his wife while I was waiting for Lorraine. He spoke to me, and I coughed, involuntarily, into his face.

- Sorry, sir,

I said,

- I couldn't help it.

- No,

he said,

- You couldn't.

My throat hurt a lot, and my lungs felt like bags of wet coal that the black dust was seeping through.

One morning, two or three weeks later, when I was half-awake, my arms folded across my desk, staring out of the window while the history master read the register, he stopped at my name.

- You're with us?
- Who, me?
- Yes, you . . . sir!
- Yes, sir,

I said,

- I am, sir.

He thumbed through the register in silence, stopped to remove his spectacles and polish them, revealing the rings around his naked eyes and a ridge on his nose, replaced them slowly and carefully, and fixed a long and icy stare on me.

- Two days last week, one the week before, three the week before that. Why?
- I was ill,

I mumbled, because I didn't have a reason, and he stood up and walked towards the window, shaking his head. He stared from the window at the cold world outside, watching a groundsman walking across the yard with a barrow to fill in a hole on the football pitch.

- If you don't pick up your ideas you are going to be left behind, lad. This is the only chance you will get,

he said.

- Are you listening to me?
- Aye, sir.
- Where were you last week?

I coughed.

- Stand up.

I pushed my desk forward, straightening my legs and my body, and pressed my fingers into the lid.

- I was ill, sir,
I lied.
- And the week before?
- I went for tests, sir ...
   I stared at my shoes and felt the skin tighten across my face.
- ... The doctor's, sir. I had to go to the hospital ...
   Atkinson, sitting at his desk behind me, laughed and pushed his ruler into the back of my legs.
- ... for an X-ray, sir.
   His face creased slightly.
- You had to go for an X-ray?
   I looked behind him at the wall.
- He thinks I have TB, sir, and I shouldn't come to school,
I lied, and coughed, embarrassed, into my hands. He stared into the air in front of him but didn't speak for a moment.
- Wait behind afterwards,
he said. His face was changed, his grey skin pulled tight over the bones, and I was worried. He put his hand on my shoulder and said,
- It will be alright, son,
and I said,
- Aye, sir.
   I knew I had touched a sore spot and I felt stupid and guilty. I lay in bed that night and listened to my breathing, and each breath burst from my lungs like a frog burping over the trenches.

   And it was worse than that, for every time he saw me in the corridors of the school he came towards me, put his hand on my shoulder and asked how I was. And I would suck in my cheeks and try to look sallow and thin like there was a bird in my lungs, clutching at the bars of my ribcage, trying to get out. I didn't know how to behave. I would say,

- Thank you, sir. I'm alright,

and try to leave. And he would grab me and say,

- Don't worry, boy,

and I would say,

- I won't, sir. Really, sir, I'm alright,

and feel his eyes follow me down the corridor, for I had seeped into his mind, like the flicker of a memory of the distant past, dust on the lungs and the pitman's cough. In assembly I would see him every morning scanning the faces until his eyes alighted on me, trying to hide from him, or coughing in the back row with hollow cheeks and a concave chest. His eyes always found me, wherever I was, and when assembly was over and the singing was done, I would dart from the hall into the yellowsmelling toilets to avoid his gaze, and wait for the bell to ring, though one day he caught me unawares as I was coming out.

- Have you heard yet?

he asked, and I looked away, shakily.

- No, sir,

and he put his hand on my shoulder, and said,

- You'll be alright,

and all I could say was,

- I've got to go, sir. Mr Johnson's waiting,

and limped off, feeling guilty that he believed me, and glad he hadn't seen through me, though his concern scared me, and his presence followed me out of the school, casting a shadow across my life. In the backstreets, in the youth club, walking down Saint Peter's Lane, I would hear his voice and see him, saying to me in a calm but worried voice,

- It will be alright, son,
and I would feel terrible.

One day I whipped off school with Lorraine. We left just
after the bell went, walking down the lane past the damp
unfriendly playing fields towards the main gate with the cold
wind in our hair, when one of the teachers came out of the
building behind us and blew his whistle. We turned and saw
him against the sky, his belly and his whistle protruding, and
we kept on walking, worrying our shoes on the wet tar, for
all the world as if we had every reason to be walking out of
school, scared to turn back and scared to run until we reached
the gate, running to leap behind a garden hedge, though we
could hear him shouting. We knew he hadn't seen our faces,
and we knew he didn't know who we were.

An old man stood in the doorway of a shed facing us. He
chewed his lip and watched us in silence.
- Poor old bugga,
I thought. He had one of those faces that looked like it had
been carved by a child, the right bits in the wrong places, and
a startled expression whatever it was he was thinking or felt.
He knew why we were there, and gestured with his hand for
us to stay where we were, on our knees in the mud, indicating
that the teacher was watching for us. And we did as he bid,
and waited, and he lit a cigarette and disappeared into the
shed. Lorraine, not believing him, followed him, crawling on
all fours. She went into the shed and I saw her face appear
through the dust of the window. She looked towards the
playing field and the school, jerked out of sight, and was
pushed out of the door by the old man, with the scrawny
strength of an old man, his muscles made of string and wire.

185

Richard Hillesley

- He's lying,
said Lorraine,
- There's no-one there.
- Bastards. You'll catch it,
said the old man. And I laughed, which only set him off.
- A'll report yis,
he shouted,
- A'll report yis to the school,
and his hand came down after us as we ran up the street, laughing. We caught a bus to Saint Cuthbert's, run with ancient soot, stripped trees bent over the gravestones. It was a windy day, and we bought saveloy dips and ate them as we walked, dipping our fingers in the onions and the gravy. She said,
- How's your chest?
- Ah.
- Well?
- Leave it be.
- It's not that serious.
- A'm not in the mood.
- Hey.
- He believes it.
- So?
- A kna. A lied.
- So?
- How do a get out of it?
- You cannot.
- Leave it.
- Tell him. Say the results are good.
   We walked past the bridges by the pit. The air was filled with the odour of wet leaves and coaldust. A man in a flying

coat cycled past. The sky clashed above us, a swirling mass of blowing clouds, slanting sunlight and shivering smoke. We walked slowly, arguing. She stopped on the corner and asked me for a ciggie. I fumbled in the pocket of my coat, which I carried over my shoulder, pulled out my packet and handed her one. I took one for myself, and lit it, cupping my hands against the wind. A car stopped beside us as I blew out the smoke, and the driver jumped out and came round behind my back. A hand reached out and grabbed the cigarette from my mouth.

- Hey.

I spun around and found myself face to face with the history master, my cigarette in his hand, his face a glaring eruption of rage, his eyes filled with something close to hate. His hand gripped my arm, so tight it was painful, and his mouth was clenched.

- Get in the car,

he said. Lorraine said,

- No.

- Get in the car.

I think she thought he would hit her, and she climbed in too. We sat in the back, caught each other's eye as he stormed around the car to the driver's seat, and were unsure whether to laugh or cry at this strange madness. This was not like him. I would expect to be paraded at assembly, made to stand on the stage while he threw sarcasms across the hall. But this was outrageous.

- You little shit,

he shouted, half turning to look at me, as the car swerved onto the wrong side of the road.

- Tuberculosis, my God,

he shouted.

- Do you know what it is?

His face that never showed emotion now smouldered with anger, his eyes spat fire, flames and hot splinters. And we cowered, silent on the back seat, avoiding his eyes in the mirror.

- I'll show you,

he said, but didn't finish his sentence.

- Aye, sir.

- Don't give me your "Aye, sirs".

The car screeched to a halt and he came round the bonnet in one movement and flung open the door.

- Get out,

and Lorraine looked to me for the reassurance I could not give her.

- Out. Both of you. Out.

We were beside the old church. He led us up the path to the graveyard. Lorraine grabbed my hand and we followed at a distance. He had stopped in front of a simple grave. It was unmarked except for an unnamed cross.

- Tuberculosis,

he said.

We stood in embarrassed silence. The wind seemed to blow messages around the stark spire and the killed trees, with their bare branches flying over the graveyard, the leaves stacked in the corners. I pulled on my coat, to keep out the sudden chill and the cold in the atmosphere. He stared at the soil in front of him, and I realised that he was as embarrassed as I was. He turned and shook his head.

- What do you think you are doing?

- Putting on me coat, sir,

I said, and he almost smiled.

- With your life, boy.

- Nothing, sir.

- That just about sums it up,

he said, and left us shamefaced between the gravestones. A falling gull spun over the roofs, and his footsteps on the gravel path echoed through the silent wind.

Richard Hillesley

Bad News from Houston

I am behind the wheel of a rental car with the radio on. The weather is hot and sticky. Lightning splits the sky. The hot air from the Gulf meets the cold wind from Alaska and brings a storm at the same time every day. I click between KPFT, KTRU and KUHT, and tap my fingers to the rhythm of the windscreen wipers clacking through the rain.

I drive smoothly and sedately and sometimes barely in control on the downtown freeways where the spray is flying and every car is trying to reach the same gap on the same horizon at the same time and no-one is in control, trucks with grinning teeth come crashing across three lanes just to cut you up, throwing up light and rain, and the guy in the rear view mirror has a face like Harry Dean Stanton and a gun in his glove compartment and is waiting for you to make a mistake so he can use it. I turn up the music and grin insanely, close my eyes and grasp the wheel. I am waiting for the crash.

I turn off down a slip road on the wrong side of the road. The rain eases off, but I know it's not over. The city is white bones and glass and casts shadows across the sky. The rain slants across the street. It's not yet dark, but the lights are coming on. A dog at the side of the road looks me over as my car glides by. It is angry and twisted in fear and snaps at me.

I stop at a gas station. I fill up, and realise the pay booth is encased in two inch thick bullet-proof glass. On the other side of the road a man is shouting at me. I can't hear what he is shouting. He shakes his fist at me. There's nothing I can say or do. I hear the word "honky" and know I am not wanted.

I drive away, playing with the map on the passenger seat.

I am looking for The Back Door Zydeco Bar. It is up a lazy road lined by trees a few miles out of the city. The road is unlit and feels like a back street in the outer reaches of Accra or Montevideo, surrounded by leftover bayous and swamps and the fading hiss and snap of cottonmouths and creepers. A smell of hot dust and ozone rises through the air as the rain comes to a stop and steam lifts in small twizzles from the puddles in the tar. The flat top is pitted with potholes.

The bar is an overgrown shack with a sign outside, lit by a fizzing lightbulb. I park on the grass, and a man in a baseball cap and a t-shirt emerges out of the shadows.
- That'll be a dollar, man,
he says.
- What for?
- To look after your car, man.
he says.
- Oh, right,
I say, and give it to him.

I can hear the music playing inside the joint, and the man on the door looks me over and shakes me down. I'm not armed. I have never held a gun in my life. The bar is a table with a plastic tablecloth pulled over it. I want a beer and she gives me a Budweiser. I don't want a Budweiser. She only has a Budweiser. I have a Budweiser.

I walk on bare ground. Half the joint is under canvas roofing, and there is no floor. The band is playing in the corner: drums, washboard, bass, guitar, singer and accordion. The singer is old, with a face that has been there and seen it all. He reaches into the depths and touches the stars. He can make you feel it in your bones. The accordion wails and rips

191

through the air and the band swings like a donkey's dick. The women are big bottomed and dance in tight sassy dresses. The dancing is sensuous and sucks me in.

In the corner there is a fan. It is big and wooden like the propeller of a fighter plane from the First World War, and is held inside a large wire cage. It's far too big and blows a stream of blasted air in a line across the room. In the stream you are blown sideways. Your hair flies off your head. Outside the stream the air is hot and sticky.

It isn't till I sit down that I feel the eyes on me and know I'm the only white face in the place. The feeling is I don't belong in here. But it's more curiosity than animosity. They want to know why I am on their territory, but I'm only here to hear the music. A big guy in a brightly coloured shirt walks towards me. He leans across my table. He isn't threatening, but I could easily take it that way.
- What you doing here, man?
he says.
- I've come for the music,
I tell him, and shrug my shoulders.
- You don't belong here, man,
he says. It isn't hostile. More like a gentle warning. I look up at him. I don't want to offend him.
- I've come for the music,
I say, and because the music's loud I shout,
- I'm English.
   His expression changes.
- Hey, man, you English? Why didn't you say?
   He reaches towards me and laughs.
- Let me buy you a drink, man.
   He buys me a drink.

- I'm Amos,

he says. He wants me to know I've found a friend.

- I'm like you,

he says.

- How's that?

- Can't you tell?

I really can't tell. I'm sure I'm like him. But I don't know what he's getting at.

- I'm Nigerian,

he says.

- Ah.

- I'm from Africa,

he says.

- Ah.

He's an alien and so am I. He drives a yellow cab, and tells me all he wants to do is to save enough money to get back to Lagos and run a taxi there.

- This place is bad, man,

he says, and I believe him.

- But you're OK?

- A job isn't everything,

he says, and I am beginning to like him. He likes to laugh, and I like his company.

- I didn't know I was black till I came to America,

he says, and grins. It's a line full of resonance and meaning and though I've heard it many times before, I haven't heard it from someone who has lived it in his bones. He nudges me and points at a white man who is sloping towards the bar, lean and slow with a left-sided walk, carrying a guitar that has travelled as far as he has.

- The folksinger,

he says. The folksinger is long and thin. His face is lived-in and vulnerable, perplexed yet knowing, as if to say life is complicated and there is no God, but he'll stick with it until something better comes along. The sadness he carries is pervasive, but he has a smile that says he's going to deal with it anyway, and you only have to look at him to see he is too far gone, but he's nobody's fool but his own. He is a friend of Amos and comes to our table. He trips against my leg and spills his whiskey onto my shirt, but he doesn't know he's done it and I brush it off. He is white and Texan but he is accepted here and gets a pat on the back and a shake of the hand from every passing man and woman.

- He drinks like other people breathe,

says Amos. When he gets up to play, the notes fall from his guitar and splinter across the floor. The songs are things of a frail and desolate beauty, naked and swept like trees in the wind. He walks you through a broken landscape of land-lords and thieves who make their beds and do not lie in them, abandoned lovers who try to make something of the beds they lie in, and relics and drifters who have no bed to lie in. He is the poet of truck stops and trailer parks and the ingenuity of the dispossessed. The songs are light and dark and drip with lost content.

- He has a white skin, but he knows what life is,

says Amos.

The notes slide through his fingers. The melodies are bright and spare. He comes in just behind the beat and you think he isn't going to make it, but he brings it back and takes you with him. The blues pour through his skin, and there isn't a word or a note that is out of place, though you can hear the whiskey on his breath and the darkness in his lungs. And when the song is over he looks out through the whiskey and the lights in wonder as they clap and cheer and whistle and are moved, and he doesn't know that he is liked, or why.

- You can try to tell him,

says Amos,

- but he won't listen unless your name is Elijah Craig or Ezra Brooks and you're a Kentucky Bourbon. The bottle is his friend, but he doesn't know that you have to own the drink, and not let it own you.

He leaves the stage and comes back to our table, unsteady on his legs, spilling onto his chair. He asks me where I'm staying, and I tell him I've found a motel where I can lie awake at night and hear the whistle of the Santa Fe and the rumble of the trains.

For a while we talk and laugh and joke. I want to know about his songs. He says he has said it all before. Once the songs were the expression of his wonder. Now the same words and tunes speak of his unease. Once he sang and drank to get high. Now he drinks and plays to obliterate himself. Amos gives him advice, but he doesn't want to hear.

He puts his bottle on the table, and tells me the story of Bobby Brown, a singer and a friend who was always on his uppers and in need of a helping hand. He lent him his favourite guitar, and Bobby took it to a pawn shop. Bobby needed the guitar to play a gig, and he needed the money to pull off a drug deal. The deal turned bad and Bobby was shot. The pawn ticket for the guitar was in the pocket of the jacket in which Bobby was buried.

On the night of the funeral he went to the grave with a bottle, a spade and a shovel, and drank to Bobby's memory. When the drinking was done, he dug into the ground to steal

195

the ticket from Bobby's jacket, and Bobby's body sat upright in its coffin. He ran for his life and didn't stop running until he hit the other side of town. The story is meant to convey a truth, but he's forgotten what that truth might be, and I don't believe a word he says.

The bottle stands before him and he stares into the abyss. He says he's tired, and he isn't talking any more. I look into his eyes and click my fingers. The story never ends and the drink goes on forever. Amos looks at me with a tear in his eye. - Stay away from him, man. He's an angel, but he's killing himself.

'Don't go to Houston, boys
Unless you have the bail,
Or the polis will arrest you,
and put you in the jail.'

I drive back to the motel along the freeway. It's three in the morning and I'm listening to the late show on KPFT and Wilfred Chevis is singing the Mona Lisa. I tap my fingers on the steering wheel and stare into the night.

The sky is clouded like the soda in a glass of whiskey and the lights are spinning past, throwing daggers at me. A truck cuts me up, big as a train, blows his horn like a sax, and the lights on his cab crackle and pop. The road is swaying and the cars race past me, and I am waiting for the crash. Their headlights rise up and down the freeway and disappear over the horizon. The blue lights of a police car flash past my shoulder. The cop looks at me sideways through the window, but he's on his way to somewhere else.

My windscreen reflects the lights and the road shines back

at me. I swerve to avoid a truck and hit the kerb. I wonder if I'm going to make it. Somehow I get there and I'm not sure how.

I crawl into bed and the mattress comes up and hits me in the face. I stare into the pillow and go out like a light.

In the morning the sun is hot and high. The light rips through the curtains. I stagger out of bed and splash some water on my face. I throw a towel around my neck and stand on the balcony of the motel. I look at the empty beer cans in the back-ends of the pick-ups parked in a line below and stretch and yawn. The whiskey is still on my breath, and the air catches my throat. I breathe deeply and stare into the white horizon, and a beat up Impala shrieks and slides into the parking lot, smoking from the rear. The driver leans out the window and shouts up at me. I am shielding my eyes from the glare of the sun and don't know who he is until he climbs out and kicks the nearside tyre. It's the folksinger, and he's waving at me.
- Come here, man,
he shouts.

I am surprised to see him and I am surprised he remembers me. I am surprised he knows where I am staying, and I am surprised he has two women with him, young and ready for life, with open faces and flowing hair. The car is rust and paint and is held together by tapes and string. I don't know where we're going, and I'm not sure I want to be going there, but I'm going anyway, and I grab a bag and jump into the car. The car bangs into life. He reverses out noisily, and we blow up a storm of dust behind us. I ask him why he has come to look for me, but it's an impulse and a whim.

Richard Hillesley

- You looked like you needed some fun,
he says. This is the way he does things. On the fly and without
a plan. He hasn't slept since last I saw him, and he has a bottle
cradled between his legs, passes it towards me but I'm not
sure I want it. He smiles but his face is tired. We draw up to
the crossing where the road crosses the Santa Fe. The lights
are flashing and the barriers are down. We have to wait for a
mile-long train, boxcars and a shaft of sunlight caught
between the couplings, boxcars and a glimpse of a truck
waiting on the other side, boxcars and a silence left behind.
- It's Sugarland bound,
he says, pointing up the track as the barrier lifts and the car
bangs into life. Boxcars rolling into the haze. They are going
round the bend and out of sight. A man in denims and a
white t-shirt leans against a tree, chews his teeth and stares
into the distance with a purpose, though he has no purpose
that I can see. The road disappears over the horizon, leaving
the city far behind. Dust in our wake, blowing up behind us.
Dust on the wind, misting up my eyes.

I ask him where we're going but he won't say. He drives
like he drinks, intensely and out of control, and the car leaps
and swerves, and the women whoop and laugh and are
friendly and put me at my ease. And the dust lifts into the sky
behind us as we turn up a lane into an avenue of trees that
disappears into a haze.

At the end of the avenue of trees is a trailer park of sorts.
Shacks and trailers and mobile homes lean at angles into the
trees above a scatter of ditches, and the ditches are filled with
yellowing roots and leaves and deadwater. Some are proud
and smart with tidy plots and picket fences. Some are worn

and tired and have seen better years. All the faces are black. Three kids are playing in the dirt with a ball. We park up the car and retire into one of the homes. One of the women makes coffee and we sit around and talk. The other woman hangs on the singer's arm. She's his wife.

- Home sweet home,

he says, and falls into a chair, and he is like he was the night before. He isn't asleep and he isn't awake. He stares into the future and talks, but the words are random and make no sense. And when he is done he gets to his feet and wanders out of the trailer. His wife follows him and I am left on my own until the other woman comes in from the kitchen. She is interested in me. My accent is exotic and she wants to talk. Her name is Rose. She has an innocence about her, driven by a high voice and a country accent of her own. She has bright eyes and smoky hair. I like her and she likes me. But I don't know where I am or how I'll find my way back.

- What's he like to live with?

I ask her and she smiles.

- Bittersweet and Bourbon,

she says, and I know what she means. We talk and laugh and eat and drink and flirt during the long afternoon until he comes back into the trailer, fresh from his bed, and waves at me with a bottle in his hand, and says,

- Follow me,

and she smiles and says,

- See you later.

- Later,

I say, and find him sitting at the edge of a ditch throwing stones at a tin can sitting on a branch on the opposite bank, a bottle of George Dickel at his side.

199

Richard Hillesley

- come here, man,
he says,
- Can you hit that can?
   I pick up a stone and hoy it across the ditch. I miss the can.
- I did this for hours when I was young,
he says,
- It's therapeutic and it's pointless. Like catching flies. You ever try to catch a fly?
- ?
- I'll keep on throwing stones until I hit it, and then I'll throw again. It's an exercise in futility,
he says, and scratches the dirt around his feet.
- Ashes to ashes, dust to dust.
he says, and passes me the bottle, but I don't want it. He smiles.
- I saw you talking to Rose,
he says.
- The first kiss is like your first glass of whiskey. You'll say you won't, but you'll fall every time. We always do.
   He smiles again.
- And if the women don't get you, the whiskey surely will.
he says and puts the bottle back to his lips. It sounds like a prophecy.

There's a crash and a gunshot. I have never heard a gunshot in my life, but I know the sound. A bullet goes ping through the branches close to my head, and I look up and see two men in the back of a pick-up with rifles and hoods over their heads. I run towards the trees and fling myself to the ground. I hear them shouting abuse and calling us motherfuckers and niggerlovers and things I've never heard before. I get to my feet and run and stumble and listen to the bullets rushing past my ears.

I fall and I'm lying on the ground gasping for breath when somebody lands on top of me. I am fighting but he's holding me down. I elbow him in the ribs, and fling him away from me. I stand up and it's Amos. I don't know where he came from.

- What you doing here, man?

he says.

- Get out.

And he drags me through the ditch and up the opposite bank. We emerge into the light and run to his car, which is waiting on the other side of the ditch, a long yellow cab hidden among the trees. He pushes me in and we drive off at speed just as the lightning breaks across the sky and the wipers begin to clack. He looks at me.

- Don't go to that place, man.

he says.

- You only go there if you're black and wanted in Louisiana.

   He looks at me.

- And you ain't black,

he says and turns on the radio. I stare out the window and the sky is dark and swirling. Lightning splits the sky, and I think about Rose.

Acknowledgements

A debt is owed to the editors of Iron Press, Prole, Fictive Dream, Storgy and CafeLit, who published early versions of stories in this collection. Special thanks go to Phil Robertson and Brett Evans of Prole and Laura Black of Fictive Dream, and to those friends who know who they are and have helped me through the years.